HEART OF A NURSE

Helen Murray

Nurse Kay Latimer had often seen and wondered about Cameron Glen, Scottish ancestral home of the Cameron-Boyds. Her curiosity led her to inspect the old manor house more closely – and to a confrontation with handsome Martin Searle, grandson of old Mrs. Cameron-Boyd. From the moment of that fateful meeting, Kay found herself drawn into a triangle in which her feelings for the two men in her life were placed in direct conflict with her duty as a nurse!

Other Large Print Books
by Helen Murray

PRESCRIPTION FOR LOVE

TO LOVE AGAIN

ISLAND OF DESIRE

AFRICAN LOVE SONG

OUTREACH

HEART OF A NURSE

Helen Murray

Curley Publishing, Inc.
South Yarmouth, Ma.

Library of Congress Cataloging-in-Publication Data

Murray, Helen.
  Heart of a nurse / Helen Murray.—Large print ed.
    p.   cm.
  1. Large type books.   I. Title.
  [PS3563.U769H4   1991]
  813'.54—dc20
  ISBN 0–7927–0696–X (large print)   90–42832
  ISBN 0–7927–0697–8 (pbk.)   CIP

Published in Large Print by arrangement with Dorchester Publishing, Inc. in the United States and Canada, the U.K. and British Commonwealth and the rest of the world market.

Distributed in Great Britain, Ireland and the Commonwealth by CHIVERS LIBRARY SERVICES LIMITED, Bath BA1 3HB, England.

Printed in Great Britain

HEART OF A NURSE

ONE

Kay Latimer paused at the top of the hill and looked back the way she had come, towards the great hall that was Braeside Clinic in the west of Scotland. Her face was glowing with health and vitality, and she peered through the deceptive curtain of lightly falling snow and saw the hall lying in its desolate position like a child's discarded model. A flake of snow settled upon her nose and she lifted a gloved hand to wipe it away, her brown eyes gleaming, her face showing her pleasure. She glanced at her companion, Dr. Kent, and saw that he was watching her, and she laughed gaily, in this last snowfall of an unrelenting winter.

"I thought you said we'd seen the last of the snow," she retorted.

"It won't lay," he promised, coming closer, clapping his gloved hands against the cold that tried to steal into his fingers. He was a short man in his middle thirties, with brown eyes and a fleshy, jovial face. He had to look up slightly to bring his gaze to Kay's eyes. "Snowdrops are out already in Matron's garden."

1

"They've been out a long time," Kay replied. She let her eyes shift from his face to the vista of desolate, bleak mountains on the horizon, beyond the huddled town of Cragton four miles away. There were still some snow patches on the mountain tops, but the warmer weather had stripped the craggy slopes of their white mantles, as if Nature intended bursting forth suddenly and without further warning into a flurry of spring activity.

It was the end of March and Kay had been working as a nursing Sister at the clinic since the end of September. She had come to Scotland from London after her mother died, and the six months of isolation and change had wrought wonders to her mental outlook. Her grief had receded sufficiently for her to take fresh interest in things about her, and now the long winter was over she was beginning to feel the tiny stirrings of hope and the reawakening of all that she had imagined was dead in her heart.

"A penny for them," Robin Kent said cheerfully. He had a deep, pleasant voice, and Kay liked the sound of it. A steady friendship had sprung up between them during her time at the Clinic, and he had helped her immensely through those black patches which had inevitably come in the dying throes of her grief.

2

"I wasn't thinking of anything in particular," she replied, meeting his gaze, a smile upon her gentle face. Her features were delicate, beautifully formed, contained in a tender oval that was framed by her rather long brown hair. Her eyes were dark and steady, a little too intense at times, but indicating her great depths, and her mouth had a generous curve which invited a second look by any man.

Robin moved closer to her, watchful, intent upon her beauty, and she smiled as she saw the expressions which crossed his fleshy face.

"Still trying to fathom out what makes me tick?" she demanded.

"I'll never be able to work that one out," he retorted. "I never tire of watching you, Kay. I adore you. I would like to call you mine, but there is an elusiveness about you that defies me. You're not in the least bit interested in me, are you?"

"Not in the way you are beginning to regard me." She let a tense seriousness occupy her tones. "I hope nothing will come along to spoil our friendship, Robin."

"I know you're not on the market for romance," he said with a wry smile. "I wouldn't injure that fragile understanding which exists between us, as much as I'd like to take you into my arms."

3

She looked anxiously into his face, knowing that he had been falling for her by slow degrees. She had watched and marked his progress, and now spring was about to unfold about them he was coming to the point where his feelings would erupt like any patient flower that had been awaiting the death of winter. It was Nature all the way, and she knew he could not help his feelings any more than she could pretend to love him where she didn't.

"I think we'd better be starting back!" He pulled back the sleeve of his thick coat and glanced at his watch. "I have an afternoon round to take care of. But can I run you into town this evening. There is a good film on that I'm sure you'd like to see."

"I had planned to stay in this evening," she said as she took his arm. There was little snow on the ground, but the surface was slippery and treacherous. The wind that tugged at them still carried a sting that brought back memories of endless days of cold and bitter weather that had commenced before Christmas.

"You stay in far too much! Why don't you let me help you out of your rut?" He broke off as his feet skidded and he almost lost his balance. Kay clutched at him, keeping him upright, and he laughed merrily as they went

4

on their uncertain way.

"It's nice and cosy in my particular rut," she said with real enthusiasm. "I'm quite happy as I am, Robin, and you might start something that will get out of hand by trying to make me go against my inclinations."

"I suppose you're right, but I just don't see why a girl as beautiful as you should be friendless and anti-social."

"I'm not as bad as that!" She showed concern that he seemed to think so. "This is an isolated spot. That's why one cannot do all the social rounds. But I don't feel a sense of loneliness. I actually enjoy this quiet life."

"It isn't for the likes of you!" He shook his head as they descended the slope. He was breathless, and he held her elbow tightly, as if afraid that they might lose their balance and finish the rest of the descent in a flurry of arms and legs. "My word! The things I do just to be in your company. You're a real outdoors girl, aren't you?"

"Not so much now as I used to be," she retorted with a smile. "And you're not keen on anything that involves effort, are you?"

"I'm much more at home with a book and a good fire, or at a sophisticated party," he admitted. "But I'll try anything once, and it does me good to get out and about. You've been a direct shock to my nature, Kay. I don't mind admitting that meeting you has made me widen my spheres of activity. But I can't contain myself any longer. I want to go on to a better understanding with you. I am hopelessly in love with you. I think you have guessed that!"

"I've noticed the signs," she said slowly. "But I don't feel the slightest compulsion to become involved with any man, Robin. My mother died last year and that put a blight upon my life. I just don't feel normal any more. I'm all alone in the world now. My father died when I was a child. I have no other family. There are two aunts on my mother's side, but I don't even know where one of them lives, and the other never bothered over me. I've become accustomed to being on my own, and I seem to have lost all interest in love."

"I understand," he said instantly. He slipped again, and almost went down on one knee. But Kay clung to him and he regained his balance. "You're still suffering from shock at your mother's death. But give yourself time, my dear girl! When spring comes you'll feel a gradual lightening of the spirit. I know what I'm talking about. Then you'll begin to feel differently. You'll come alive again, like a tulip in a garden." He smiled as he met her

6

frank gaze. "You're making me feel poetical," he accused.

"I like you so very much," she said, under pressure from some obscure emotion. "You've never attempted to intrude upon my personal life, Robin. Another man would have at least attempted to kiss me, but you've respected my feelings, and you've done a great deal to help me over my grief."

"There you are," he declared. "That proves I've been working in the right direction. At least we have become very good friends. I suppose that is progress, in a way."

They were nearing the bottom of the hill, and soon they clambered over a stile that gave access to the grounds of the Clinic. The path they followed wound across a meadow, and crossed a gurgling stream by way of a rough wooden bridge. They passed under some gaunt looking trees that were showing signs of buds already, and passed through a kitchen garden that boasted of nothing more than a few sorry looking cabbages. When they reached the cobbled yards at the rear of the Clinic, Robin paused and gripped Kay's elbow with strong fingers.

"Don't worry about the way my feelings are progressing," he said. "I'd hate for you to have second thoughts now because of my love for you. I'll never bother or worry you

7

with my feelings. If a miracle happened and you fell in love with me then I'd be only too happy to reciprocate."

"You're such a thoughtful person," she murmured.

"You're the only one who counts," he replied firmly.

They parted just inside the back door, Robin going up to his quarters on the top floor and Kay divesting herself of her coat and going along the wide corridor to the massive kitchen, where she opened the door and peered inside for Mrs. Rawdon, the cook. She saw the tall, thin woman by the roaring fire across the room, and entered to cross to her side. Of all the people who worked at the Clinic, Mrs. Rawdon appealed most to Kay, and the strange feeling of attachment seemed mutual.

"Kay, I saw you up on the hill with Dr. Kent! It beats me how you like going out in that cold weather. Even when there was snow on the ground you wrapped up and went out."

"It isn't cold today, Mrs. Rawdon!" Kay stretched out her hands towards the blazing fire, and she smiled as she caught the older woman's eye.

Mrs. Rawdon shook her head. She was a pleasant woman who had been employed

8

as cook from the founding of the Clinic. Widowed, she had no family, and had taken to Kay from the first, upon hearing of Kay's bereavement. Kay had come to look upon this homely woman as a second mother, and in the six months of their friendship they had accepted the strange fact that they were close friends despite the disparity in their ages and outlook. They occasionally went into nearby Cragton, shopping together and sitting in the restaurant for tea or coffee, making much of the simple outings, for such was the way of life in these remote parts. Mrs. Rawdon took a keen interest in Kay's activities, no matter what they were, and it was she who had first opened Kay's eyes to the fact that Robin Kent was falling in love with her.

"How are you getting along with Doctor Kent?" Mrs. Rawdon asked, peering at Kay with faded blue eyes. She was sixty-one years old, and had spent her lifetime in the service of others. She'd never had a home of her own, having always been employed in one big house or another. Her husband had been a butler in his lifetime, and there had never been a need for a home of their own.

"He's good company." Kay moved nearer the fire, her eyes glinting in its bright reflection. "He's certainly helped me through the winter."

"Are you in love with him?" Mrs. Rawdon asked the question with no awkwardness in her gentle tones.

"No." Kay shook her head, and her eyes showed a momentary doubt. "He knows that, too."

"But he's in love with you, Kay."

"I know. He told me so."

"You make an ideal couple. You seem very well suited."

"Except that I don't love him."

"You never know what may turn up." Mrs. Rawdon smiled as she moved to the stove. "I expect you could do with a nice cup of tea after your walk, couldn't you?"

"Yes please!" Kay pulled a chair to one side of the fire and sat down. She felt the radiant heat envelop her, and a shiver seemed to course sinuously through her. She thought of Robin Kent, and felt a half-wish that she could find something in her heart for him. But he just didn't measure up to her ideal of a man. She had no inclination towards romance, and it would need a very good man indeed to change her present attitude. It wasn't just the death of her mother that had alienated her sense of romance from the conscious part of her mind. She had been let down once, by someone who had at the time been very close to her, but she had not

10

suffered unduly from the setback. All the incident had done was to make her more thoughtful and she never suffered heartbreak because she had told herself instantly that she had not been really in love.

"What are you thinking about?" Mrs. Rawdon's voice sounded a long way off, and Kay started a little as she jerked herself from her thoughts.

"Nothing in particular." Kay smiled as she took the cup of tea that was offered to her. "Thank you!" She stirred the tea thoughtfully.

"You're always thinking of nothing in particular!" Mrs. Rawdon said. "When are you going to find yourself someone you can love?"

Such was the friendliness between them that the question did not seem an invasion of Kay's privacy, and she smiled as she shook her head.

"I'm not romantically inclined, so I doubt if I shall ever fall in love. I'll leave that to the other girls here."

"Well, I won't say that I agree with your outlook, but you do know your own mind best!" Mrs. Rawdon sipped her tea and regarded Kay with watchful eyes. "But you are all alone in the world, Kay, and you are twenty-eight. If you intend ever to find a husband then it's not too soon to start looking."

"Around here?" Kay laughed musically. "The only thing I might have met around Cragton this winter was an abominable snowman."

They both laughed merrily, and Kay, watching the the older woman's face, could not help wondering how it was that people could put their troubles behind themselves and appear to the rest of the world as if nothing had happened. But she had done the same sort of thing over the death of her mother! Time helped. Time was the greatest healer of them all. She caught her breath as a pang of wistfulness touched her mind. She tried to shrug it off, knowing that if she gave any black mood half a chance she would be swamped by despair in no time at all.

"I'd better start thinking of tea," Mrs. Rawdon said. "I expect you're hungry after your walk."

"It has given me an appetite," Kay admitted.

"What are you doing this evening?"

"I have been asked to go into town, but I don't really feel like going."

"What will you do if you stay here?"

"Sit and read, I shouldn't wonder."

"I expect you've read every book there is in

the Clinic library!"

"Just about. But with spring coming, and lighter evenings on the way, I shall spend a great deal of my time walking across the moors."

"Just you be careful where you set foot around here," Mrs. Rawdon warned. "The moors are very deceptive, and it would be too easy for you to get lost. If a mist closes in about you then you could die of exposure out there."

"I wouldn't go too far," Kay said quickly. "But I have noticed a very old house standing at the foot of a hill about four miles away. It's quaint, and I should like to look at it more closely. Ever since I first saw it before Christmas I've had a yearning to see it in more detail."

"You won't be able to get inside."

"Really?" Kay was struck by Mrs. Rawdon's stern voice.

"It belongs to old Mrs. Cameron-Boyd. She won't let anyone near the place since the local authorities have tried to buy her out. There's talk of a reservoir being built in these parts, and the most suitable spot is the valley where the house stands. It's called Cameron Glen, by the way."

"Does she live there alone?"

"Except for a grandson and a few servants,

people who have been with her for a great many years. The old lady must be nearly ninety now!"

"Poor old soul! She doesn't need to be worried by that sort of thing at her age!" There was genuine concern in Kay's voice.

"She's a tough old bird, Kay," Mrs. Rawdon told her with a laugh. "She took a shotgun to one of the ministry men who tried to talk to her."

"That sounds like evidence of old Highland spirit."

"And not the kind that comes out of a bottle either," Mrs. Rawdon said, laughing. "But I know the cook at Cameron Glen and if you are really interested in looking around the place then no doubt we could arrange for you to visit."

"It would be interesting. The house looks as if it's hundreds of years old."

"It's got quite a history to it," Mrs. Rawdon agreed. "But I didn't know you were interested in that sort of thing, although, on second thoughts, I suspect it is just the subject to interest you."

"You're quite right. I'm in my highest delight when I can look around old buildings."

"Is that why you're so happy here?" Mrs. Rawdon demanded.

"Partly. I like it here because it's so remote. It's totally different to anything I've ever been accustomed to, and I hope I can stay here for the rest of my nursing career."

"Is that the sum total of your ambitions?" Mrs. Rawdon shook her head slowly. "What do you really want, Kay?"

"Out of life?" Kay shrugged as she considered. "That's difficult to say, really. I've never given it much thought. I suppose I'm perfectly happy with my work, and so long as I can do that then ambition doesn't really matter. My ambition is to just keep on working."

"I'll never know what makes your kind of girl tick, Kay. I've seen a great many nurses come and go here. Some stick it for months, and some can't take it more than a few weeks, but whatever they've done, they've all had the same inner fire. Nursing is a thankless task."

"Is that what you think, despite your close connections with the Clinic?" Kay smiled slowly, shaking her head as she looked into the older woman's pale eyes. "Mrs. Rawdon, one doesn't need thanks in this business. We get our thanks from seeing sick people get well again. It's enough to know that people rely on us and that we can actually help them."

"You have to be born to the job."

"I expect so. We do get a lot of dirty jobs, and routine work can become dreary. But it's the principle behind nursing that really counts."

"You've certainly found your niche in life. But if you hadn't become a nurse, what else would you have done?"

"I've never thought about it. I've wanted to be a nurse ever since I've been old enough to know about nursing."

The door opened and Matron entered, bringing their conversation to an abrupt end. Kay set down her cup and saucer and got to her feet, almost reluctant to leave the heat of the fire. The quarters were heated by radiators, but it was always nice, to Kay's mind, to see an open fire.

Matron, Miss Margaret Stokes, was a tall, slender woman of fifty-two who looked at least ten years younger with her carefully attended black hair which showed little trace of the years that had passed her by. She paused on the threshold of the kitchen and smiled when she saw Kay.

"Hello, Sister," she called. "Do you enjoy running about over the local landscape in a blizzard?"

"It was hardly that, Matron," Kay replied with a laugh.

16

"Well, that's what it looked like from the window of my office. I wouldn't have been up there in your boots for anything in the world."

"It takes all sorts to make a world, Matron," Mrs. Rawdon said, nodding wisely. "But I'll stay down here with you while Kay runs about communing with Nature, even if she does it with a nice young man like Dr. Kent."

Kay felt her cheeks grow hot, and she moved to the door. She knew that in a small community such as the Clinic, there would be a certain amount of speculation about any of the staff pairing off, but she didn't want anyone jumping to conclusions about her association with Robin Kent. She could never get serious about Robin, and she knew it. More, she wanted everyone else to know it.

"Don't let my arrival chase you away, Sister," Miss Stokes said.

"I was about to go up to my room, anyway, Matron. But I do spend a lot of my off duty time in here with Mrs. Rawdon."

"One has to find company where one can," Miss Stokes said. "But I want to have a chat with you, Sister. We have a new nurse starting duty on Monday and I'm thinking of putting her with you. She's a very good

17

nurse, by all accounts, but she's had some bad luck recently and this has affected her nerves. She lost a perfectly good job at a General hospital in Liverpool because of the state of her nerves, and she's only coming with us because she has some connection with one of our directors. As you are our most sympathetic Sister I'm thinking of putting her under your wing. Would you take care of her?"

"Certainly. I'll do what I can to help her. But why did she lose her job in Liverpool? We're not likely to have any trouble with her, are we? I mean, she'll be able to do her duties properly. Shall we be able to trust her with the patients?"

"I think so, but watch her carefully for a few days to see how she shapes. We're only taking her on trial, and I'll rely on your judgement when we make a report on her."

"Very well, Matron." Kay nodded as she left the kitchen, and her thoughts were filled with speculation as she went up the back stairs to her quarters.

They couldn't afford to carry a passenger on the staff, no matter what influence might have been wielded to get the newcomer her position at Braeside. But Kay would be very fair, and she had already made up her mind

18

to help where she could. People had to help one another! That was the main reason they were put on the earth! At least, that was Kay's personal philosophy and she had always stuck to it. But she had some misgivings where the patients were concerned. One could not be too careful about the people who came into contact with the patients. If a nurse had lost her job at a hospital, no matter the reason, then engaging her at the Clinic might well mean that a certain amount of trouble would arise from the fact . . .

TWO

The week-ends were always lonely at Braeside, and this despite the fact that a great many visitors came to see the patients on Saturdays and Sundays. There were no fixed visiting hours. Visitors could call at any reasonable time. But the Clinic was run with a token staff to enable the others to take advantage of the week-end, and Kay never really worried if she drew duty or not. While there were books in the Clinic library which she hadn't read then she was satisfied.

But this week-end found her off duty, and

Robin Kent had gone home for the day to visit his parents living in Carlisle. He had plagued Kay to go with him, using all manner of arguments to support his case, but she refused to agree or accept. When he had gone she felt a momentary pang of regret that she had not tried to make his week-end happier, but she had no wish to become involved any deeper with him. No doubt his parents would jump to conclusions if she had gone home with him, and she didn't want to add complication, involvement, or any degree of hope to Robin's outlook.

On Saturday afternoon, with nothing to do but entertain herself, Kay dressed warmly and set out to take a closer look at the house known as Cameron Glen. The afternoon was bright despite the cold wind, and she walked briskly along the path that led in the general direction of the house. She was in no hurry, but she knew it would take her a considerable time to reach the house. Her thoughts were gentle as she paced herself over the long hike, and her feet swished in the wet grass. The air was bracing, and the weak sun did its best to show a foretaste of coming spring.

The path seemed to have a mind of its own, and the ground played tricks with itself, never level and always uneven. There were shallow pools of water lying in the depressions, and

Kay had to skirt them in order to keep her feet dry in her sturdy boots. But she enjoyed the wide open spaces and walked on and on, carrying with her the knowledge that she was mistress of her own life and that whatever happened, she would have only herself to blame for any mistake which she might make.

She considered Robin Kent as she walked, her mind settling on him as the subject most likely to give her something to think about. She searched her mind for any emotion which she might feel for him, but the deepest analysis could not produce a spark of love. She had to admit that she could never love him.

The loneliness of the moors appealed to her, and she strode out purposefully, keeping in the general direction of her destination by catching a glimpse of the town in the distance and making sure that it was always on her left. She reached some high ground, and for the first time the big house that she wished to see more closely appeared before her, but still a long way off. When she looked back the way she had come she could see the Clinic standing in its lofty and solitary spot, and her awareness of the rugged beauty of this area gave her great pleasure.

Silence pressed in about her like heavy drapes, and she relished the knowledge that

21

there was probably not another person within a mile of her. She went on, leaving the path now the big house was plainly in view, and her feet stumbled over rough ground and splashed through shallow stretches of water.

It was a joy to be alive and out in the open air. Although her face felt cold, Kay knew it was filled with colour. She swung her arms and went on happily, uncaring of the moist conditions and certain that she would be able to return to the Clinic before nightfall.

When she came to a fence that enclosed the outer grounds of Cameron Glen, Kay paused and looked around. This was private property. The knowledge disconcerted her for a moment, but she had come a long way to look at the house and she didn't fancy turning away with her curiosity unappeased. She gingerly climbed over the fence, careful not to catch herself on the barbed wire, and then she went on blithely, walking straight towards the big house. On her right now a rising slope of arid ground rose up and up to a rocky apex, and it seemed to menace the house with its gigantic crown. Rocks were piled upon rocks in jumbled fashion, as if an angry giant of some long ago era had stacked them out of his way. There were some highland cattle grazing on the hillside, and Kay looked around fearfully, filled with a townswoman's healthy respect for any large animal.

She found a path and followed it, and came eventually to a low stone wall that separated kitchen gardens from the pasture. She paused and looked long and hard at the house, finding it larger than she had imagined, and she walked around the outer perimeter of the grounds to view it from all angles.

The sun had disappeared behind a bank of ominously dark clouds, although Kay did not notice it in her interest of the house. Her first intimation that the weather was conspiring against her came with a large drop of rain on her cheek. She lifted a hand to wipe her face, and glanced up at the lowering sky. The next instant a heavy shower descended, and she stood in the open, unable to take shelter. The shower passed in a matter of moments, but her coat was soaked and she felt chilled. With a rueful smile on her face, she started around the house, intending to find her path. She could see the Clinic in the distance, and there was a long return walk before her.

The barking of a dog attracted her attention and she paused by the corner of a small copse, frowning a little as she imagined being chased by a guard dog. Then she saw movement just inside the trees, and the next instant a man wearing dark clothes, his feet pushed into

23

gumboots, appeared and paused to stare at her. A large black and white dog came to his side and flopped down on the wet ground.

"Good afternoon," Kay called in anxious tones.

"Good afternoon," came the instant reply, but the man did not move or show any friendliness. He had a gun under one arm, and a flat cap was pulled low over his forehead shadowing his eyes.

"I suppose I'm really trespassing here." Kay felt some explanation was due, for she was miles from any beaten track. "I'm from the Clinic over there. I've often seen this old house from a distance, and I've been planning to come and take a closer look." Her brown eyes were narrowed as she watched him for reaction, and she saw some of the tension go out of his features.

"It was a foolish thing to do, crossing the moors dressed like that at this time of the year." He came forward then, approaching quickly, and Kay saw that he was a young man, tall and heavily built, with fair hair showing at his temples. His eyes were blue, narrowed now as he looked at her searchingly, and he was strikingly handsome. But there was something of a sullen expression on his face, as if he instinctively resented her intrusion upon this private property.

"You think I'm not suitably dressed?" she demanded.

"You're soaked to the skin, aren't you?"

"I admit I didn't allow for the rain. But I thought it would have kept fine."

"And you're going to walk back across the moors to the Clinic, are you?" He glanced at his wristwatch. "You'll never get back before dark."

Kay glanced around, and she saw with some surprise that already the afternoon was turning gloomy, but that could be on account of the rain clouds building up in the sky.

"You'd better come to the house with me and let your coat dry out before you catch pneumonia. The wind will cut right through you."

"But if I delay now I shan't get back to the Clinic before nightfall," she protested.

"I'll drive you back when you're dry." His tones gave her the impression that he wouldn't be refused, and she watched his face keenly as he stared at her. "Come along," he said sharply. "When you're wet like that you should keep moving. If you're not careful you're going to be a patient at your precious Clinic."

There was an odd note in his voice, and Kay frowned as she fell into step at his side and walked with him back towards the house.

The dog trotted along at his heels, and she could not help noticing how it obeyed even his slightest glance.

"Perhaps I'd better introduce myself," he said in grudging tones. "I'm Martin Searle!" He said it as if he expected her to know him. When she made no reply he said: "I'm Mrs. Cameron-Boyd's grandson. I take care of the estate."

"Mrs. Cameron-Boyd is the owner of the house!" Kay remembered that Mrs. Rawdon had mentioned the old lady who refused to sell to the local authority.

"That's right." He spoke stiffly, as if he resented answering her. They entered a garden through a side gate and crossed to a terrace, and Kay felt awkward when they paused before the massive front door. She was conscious of her wet coat and muddy boots. But he opened the door and stepped aside for her. "In you go," he said in rising tones when she remained standing.

"But my feet! They're muddy."

"So are mine! I usually stand on the mat inside the door to take off wet shoes, not out here where the concrete is wet!"

She took a deep breath and entered the house, waiting for him to follow her, and when he had closed the door he stooped and pulled off his boots. When he straightened he looked at her, for she was still standing upright, watching him.

"Get your coat off, and then sit down on that chair and take off your boots."

She obeyed him because there seemed nothing else she could do. Then she heard a door close nearby and looked around to see a tall silver-haired old man coming towards them. She removed her coat and the newcomer held out his hand for it without comment. Kay sat down on the nearby chair and tugged off her fur-lined boots, and she discovered that her feet were wet as well. She looked up to find Martin Searle staring at her, and he nodded slowly when he caught her eye.

"Your feet are wet too. Better get those stockings off." He turned to the waiting servant. "Angus see that Miss –!" He paused and looked at Kay. "You didn't tell me you name!" he accused.

"Kay Latimer."

"Angus, see that Miss Latimer's coat is dried, and take her boots as well."

He paused while the manservant took Kay's coat and boots and departed, his eyes on Kay's feet. She could feel the intensity of his gaze, and a strange feeling of awkwardness came to her. He took off his cap, and she could see his face clearly for the first time. He was handsome. That much she divined in one searching glance. But his manner was abrupt, as if meeting her and having to help her was too much trouble.

"Would you like some tea?" he demanded. "You'll have to wait until your coat has dried." Once more he glanced at her feet, and Kay looked down at her wet stockings. "Come into this room. You'll find it cosy, and you can take off those stockings and place them near to the fire to dry."

He crossed the hall as he spoke, and Kay followed him, aware that her wet feet were leaving damp marks on the highly polished wooden floor. The room they entered was large and high, with tall windows at the end overlooking a stretch of sodden lawn. It was a study, she judged, glancing at a desk and the bookshelves on one wall, and there was a blazing fire in a large grate. He pulled forward an easy chair for her, then turned to leave.

"Put your stockings in the hearth to dry," he commanded. "I'll organize some tea."

"You're very kind," Kay ventured. "But there's no need to go to all this trouble for me."

"We have an unwritten law in these parts." His tones were still gruff, but the edge had gone from them. "We always help anyone in trouble on the moors."

"But I'm not in trouble on the moors. I

28

have a three-mile walk in front of me, and if I don't get started soon I shall be in the dark before I get back to the Clinic."

"I've already told you that I'll drive you back to the Clinic!" The sharpness was back in his tones. He glared at her for a moment, then turned away. "I'll be back in a few minutes," he said as he went off. "Get those stockings off and warm your feet."

She waited until he had closed the door before going to the fire, and she shivered involuntarily as she got within the radius of heat. Taking off her stockings, she spread them not too close to the fire, and then sat down and pushed her feet towards the heat. She sighed and relaxed, glancing around the room with interest. The feeling of awkwardness remained with her. He could have concealed his impatience at having to help her, she thought remotely, and there was a picture of his face in her mind. Martin Searle! His name was on her lips. Had she ever heard of him? She didn't think so, and she sighed heavily as she spread her long fingers towards the leaping flames.

Minutes later he returned, and he had changed out of his outdoor clothes and was wearing brown trousers and a high-necked thick sweater.

"Feeling warmer?" he demanded, looking

into the hearth where steam was rising from her stockings.

"Yes thank you!" She tensed a little as he came across to the fire and spread his hands to the glow. She was conscious of her long legs stretched out towards the fire, but the heat on her bare toes was wonderful, and she took a deep breath and sighed inaudibly. Looking up at him, she saw he was watching her, and there was a hardness in his blue eyes.

"I'm so sorry to be so much bother to you," she ventured.

"Who said you're a bother?"

"Well, I must be." She wasn't going to admit that his harsh manner had been all too obvious. "I could have walked back to the Clinic without too much trouble."

"Don't let's go into that again." He glanced at the clock on the heavy mantelpiece. "Tea will be brought in shortly. We'll have to take it in here because Grandmother wouldn't be too pleased if she knew there's a stranger in the house."

Kay drew her feet back a little from the fire. She was comfortably warm now, and felt cosy after the cold afternoon. There was a tap at the door before an awkward silence descended upon them, and when he strode forward to open it a maid appeared carrying a large tray. Behind the maid came Angus, the servant, and he was carrying a pair of women's slippers.

"Would you care to put these on until your boots are dried, Miss?" There was a half smile on the man's face as he paused before her.

"Thank you!" Kay was only too aware of her bare feet. She felt at a disadvantage without footwear, and hurriedly pushed her feet into the slippers.

"They're mine, Miss," the maid said, smiling as she set down the tray on a small table on the other side of the fireplace.

"Thank you!" Kay smiled at the girl.

"I've seen you around town sometimes." There was no fear of Martin Searle in the maid's manner, and Kay was a little surprised by the fact. She had gained impressions of this man who had spoken so harshly to her, and she wouldn't have been surprised had he taken up a whip to deal with his staff. "You're from the Clinic, aren't you?" the maid went on, pouring tea while she glanced at Kay.

"I'm a Sister there," Kay replied and could not prevent her gaze from lifting to Martin Searle's face.

"That will do, Kitty," he said stiffly to the maid. "I'll carry on from there."

"Yes, sir." The girl smiled at Kay and turned away, followed out by the servant, and when the door closed behind them Martin

Searle bent over the tray. He glanced at Kay.

"Sugar?" he demanded.

"One spoonful please." She watched him as he picked up a spoon. He was obviously one of the strong silent type, but there was a harshness to his manner that didn't seem to fit in with his general appearance. She noticed tiny lines at the corners of his eyes, and thought they were laughter lines. Altogether his expression was too formal and closed. "Thank you." She took the cup and saucer from him, noting how strong and powerful his hands were, and she relaxed in her seat and watched him as he sat down opposite.

"So you're a Sister at the Clinic!" He spoke in low tones. "How long have you been there?"

"About six months."

"Where do you live? Rather, where is your home?"

"I come from London originally."

"What makes you want to be buried in such a remote spot. Are you trying to forget something, or someone?" He was trying to be sociable, but he asked his questions in the manner of a policeman talking to a prime suspect.

"I came here because my mother died last year, and I thought a job among strangers would help me get over her death."

There was a short silence while he stared at her, and Kay watched his face. He sighed rather heavily and moved impatiently in his seat, then took up his tea and sipped slowly.

"I'm sorry! I shouldn't have asked that question. Forgive my curiosity, but I couldn't help wondering why such a beautiful girl as yourself would want to bury herself alive. It must have been a long winter for you."

"I don't mind the loneliness. I was never one for the bright lights." She smiled faintly as she gazed into the leaping flames. Her youth seemed so far away and all the joys and pleasures of being young had been curtailed by her need to study.

"Are you intending to stay long at Braeside? I understand that most of the nurses who come there leave after a few weeks, and very few stay as long as a year."

"I'll stay as long as they want me. I have nowhere to go back to in London."

"No family?" He sounded surprised.

"None at all." She could not prevent a catch sounding in her voice, and she firmed her lips for a moment. She looked up to meet his gaze, and found his blue eyes studying her intently.

"You must lead a very lonely sort of life. What do you do with yourself when you're off duty?"

"There's plenty to do," she retorted. "I read a lot. The weather hasn't been fit for a dog to go out, especially in the evenings. But now the nights are getting lighter I expect to do a lot of tramping around the moors. I like that kind of activity."

"Let me give you a word of warning. Be very careful on the moors. You'd be greatly surprised to know just how many people get into trouble out there. Treat the moors with respect and you won't go far wrong." His tones were mellowing slowly, and now his face seemed inclined towards friendliness. But there was still a stiffness in his manner.

"Well I didn't think I would get into any trouble this afternoon. I could see the Clinic every time I turned around."

"And if the mist had suddenly closed in?" His eyes were holding her gaze, and Kay studied the angle of his jaw. She saw that he had small, very neat ears, and his nose was tip-tilted. His face was one that immediately registered itself in her mind, and she knew without having to consider it that she liked him, and that despite his brusque manner.

She didn't answer his question about the mist. Right now she didn't feel the least like walking across the moors. She leaned towards the fire, her face suddenly serious, her hands held out to the blaze.

34

"Will you stay to tea and let me drive you back to Braeside later this evening?"

She looked up at him. There was sudden appeal in his voice. He was watching her intently, and there seemed to be a pleading expression on his face.

"That's if you've nothing better to do," he added.

"But your grandmother," she said.

"If I introduce you as a friend of long standing then she won't mind. You did say you have nothing much to do on your time off. If you're so interested in the house that you walked nearly four miles just to look at the exterior, then the least I can do is show you around inside."

"Thank you, that's very kind. I would like to stay, if I won't be in the way."

He smiled, and his face was transformed. She watched him closely, relieved that the last vestiges of impatience had fled from his features. He seemed a lot younger now, and she was struck by the attractive quality about him. She hadn't met a more handsome man. He had one of those kind of faces that a girl had to give a second look to.

"It can't be very pleasant for you at Braeside in the evenings," he went on, as if trying to convince himself that she must be lonely when off duty. "Do the week-ends drag when you've nothing to do?"

"I'm never in the unhappy position where I have nothing to do," she countered, watching his face.

"But you're off duty now, and all you've done is walk across the moors." He frowned then, and she saw it, her face expressionless as she watched the changes crossing his features. "Has no one warned you that it could be dangerous on the moors for other reasons than the ones I explained to you?"

"What do you mean?"

"There are some unsavoury types about who might welcome the chance to encounter an unaccompanied girl out there."

She shivered at the thought, but she forced a smile, and appeared unconcerned.

"I've never heard any talk that a girl might be molested."

"Well, there's always the first time. You'd better be careful in future."

She nodded, and for some reason her mind was working upon other thoughts about him. Was he married? Surely his wife would have put in an appearance if he were. But he didn't have the married look about him. But there had to be a girl somewhere in his life. A man as handsome as he would have a whole flock of girls interested in him.

He was watching her again. She wondered

if he found her as attractive as she was finding him. Her breast seemed to fill with fluttery sensation, and she caught her breath and held it for a moment before releasing it silently. For six months she had been in this locality, and hadn't known that a man such as he existed. The thought made her realise that hers was a lonely life, and for a short time, while she held her breath and wondered, she became aware that she was missing the companionship that a girl could find with company. But then her habit of holding communion with herself took over again and she forced away the betraying impulses. She didn't need anyone. She had been on her own for a considerable time and she would remain on her own.

"Feeling warmer now?" he enquired. "You're looking as if you've thawed out. I'm sorry I was angry with you when I first met you, but when I saw you it seemed as if you had committed an unpardonable crime by being out on the moors as you were. If you had seen some of the people I've helped recover from that desolation out there you wouldn't venture more than half a mile from the Clinic without a guide."

"I see. Of course, ignorance is no excuse, is it? But this afternoon seemed so nice, and after being practically cooped up all winter, it seemed like a good idea to get out and about."

She watched his face, seeing a further breakdown in his stiff manner. Now he seemed almost human, and she warmed a little to him. He was the first stranger she had spoken to in six months, and it was refreshing to look upon an unknown face and to hear a strange voice. There was a sudden longing inside her that she tried to cut short almost before it made its presence known. But her pleasant train of thought was interrupted by the door of the room being thrown open suddenly, and when she looked around she saw a small, incredibly old woman standing on the threshold.

For a moment there was a startled silence in the room, and Kay found herself under surveillance by a pair of still youthful brown eyes that stared at her from a mass of wrinkles. She didn't need to be told this was his grandmother, Mrs. Cameron-Boyd, and she wondered at the suspicion showing in the old lady's face. Before Martin could move or speak, his grandmother came forward with quick, nervous strides, pausing before Kay and peering down at her like a hawk surveying prospective prey.

"And who is this, Martin?" she demanded in high pitched tones. "Is she another of those people sent by the Ministry? Has she come

38

here to spy on me?"

Kay moistened her lips, embarrassed and not a little perturbed by the fierce expression in the old lady's face and eyes. The spirit of the Highlands was personified in this small, old but agile lady, and Kay didn't know quite what to expect as she awaited developments.

THREE

"Grandmother, this is Sister Kay Latimer from Braeside Clinic!" Martin got quickly to his feet and came forward to make the introductions. "Kay, this is my grandmother, Mrs. Cameron-Boyd. Kay was attracted by the sight of Cameron Glen, Grandmother, and she walked over from the Clinic. She was on her way back when I saw her, and a good thing too, because it would have been dark before she got off the moors."

"A nursing Sister!" Those bird-like brown eyes studied Kay intently. "You ought to have had more intelligence, young woman, wandering about on the moors. Didn't anyone tell you better?"

"I'm afraid I didn't think there could possibly be any trouble," Kay said.

"And you got wet, and your feet were wet!" Those old brown eyes didn't miss a detail. "You would have been a patient at the Clinic if you'd walked back there."

"That's exactly what I told her, and why I brought her in," Martin said, and Kay saw a faint smile on his lips. But his face showed her encouragement, and Kay began to breathe a little easier. She'd begun to have visions of being run off the place with a shotgun. Mrs. Rawdon had told her a thing or two about this remarkable old Highland lady.

"Have you had tea yet?" Mrs. Cameron-Boyd moved to the seat that Martin had vacated, and she seated herself carefully, her eyes watching Kay all the time. Her eyes were the only feature about her that seemed alive, animated, and they held Kay's dark eyes like a magnet attracting metal.

"I was waiting for you," Martin told her, seating himself upon an arm of her chair and placing a hand affectionately upon her thin, bowed shoulders.

"We don't very often have guests here, my dear!" Mrs. Cameron-Boyd smiled gently, and her face was transformed from harshness to pleasure.

"You don't encourage visitors as a rule, Grandmother," Martin put in, winking at Kay. He seemed to have changed his manner completely now, and Kay felt a pang of warm regard for him. She might so easily have missed him this afternoon, and she wouldn't have missed any of this for anything in the world.

"There are visitors and visitors," his grandmother said in her sharp tones. "But someone like you, Sister, would always be welcome here. We lead a very lonely life."

"You have only yourself to blame for that," Martin went on. "Just think of the times I try to get you to put on your Sunday best and go out with me!"

"I don't like going out. This is my house and I'm going to stay in it until I die. If I go out there's no telling who might sneak in and take over."

"I keep telling you that the authorities can't do that without an order." He smiled at Kay. "You can't explain anything to Grandmother," he added. "She thinks she's still in the last century. She even took a shotgun to someone from one of the local authority departments when they came to tell her that this valley is to be made into a reservoir."

"Two hundred years this estate has been in our family. Two hundred years! Now they want to drown it! They're going to flood everything!" The old lady's eyes glinted

41

with fierce determination. "Not while there's breath in my body. Do you hear? I shan't be able to rest easy in my grave if they take this place away from us."

"There's still a chance that they'll select another site," Martin said. "But nothing has been settled yet." He looked at Kay as he explained. "Grandmother always looks on the black side."

"That's why I'm never disappointed when bad things happen," came the quick retort. "Isn't tea ready yet, Martin? I do believe it gets later day by day. Give them a ring and tell them to hurry it up. It's not right that we should keep our guest waiting. Have you shown her over the house yet? If she's interested in the outside then she ought to be given the chance to look around in here. This place isn't what it used to be a hundred years ago. Even when I was a child it was different. It's been let down in the past twenty years. Perhaps I ought to let them flood it. We can't afford to keep it up any longer."

"There's no need to talk like that, and let Kay go away with odd impressions of us," Martin said slowly. "You know why we haven't spent any money on the upkeep, and it isn't because we can't afford it. There's been rumours about this valley being flooded for as long as I can remember, and it wouldn't

42

be sense to spend a sizeable fortune on doing the place up if it is to be flooded."

"Money has no interest for me at my time of life," the old lady said sharply. "But I would like to see the house restored to how I remember it as a girl. I could die easily if I knew the old place was going on after I departed."

"Don't get morbid now." Martin got to his feet and walked towards the door. "Keep Kay entertained while I slip along to the kitchen."

He left the room and Kay turned her attention to Mrs. Cameron-Boyd, to find the old lady watching her intently.

"May I ask how old you are, my dear?"

"I'm twenty-eight!" Kay smiled.

"I wish I were twenty-eight again. But where do you come from?"

Kay explained, and the old lady drew her out gradually, asking a host of pertinent questions about her background and former life. Kay answered cheerfully and wholeheartedly. She liked this incredible old lady.

"You do such wonderful work in your particular job," Mrs. Cameron-Boyd said. "I have always admired nurses. If I hadn't been so fortunate in life I would have been a nurse."

"Nursing was very much harder upon

nurses in the days when you might have been in the profession," Kay said gently.

"From what I read in the papers, I'd say they still haven't brought conditions wholly up to date," came the quick reply. "You must tell me all about the Clinic. Will you come and see me again?"

"I'd love to." Kay nodded as she spoke. "I do get a lot of time on my hands."

"Well, I don't expect Martin will ask you here again. He can't abide girls around the place. But I would like to talk to you. I like your face. You're a dedicated girl, I can tell that. You're not like these modern young women who demand everything and want to give nothing in return. But you're not to walk across the moors again without company. When you wish to come and see me then telephone here and I'll have Martin come and pick you up."

"Thank you. I shall look forward to coming again." Kay did not add that she felt happy because she knew that coming again would mean seeing more of Martin Searle. There was a warm glow inside her that had nothing to do with the heat from the fire. Her eyes were sparkling as she watched the old lady's intent face.

"I shall expect you to come, so don't get the idea that you can go away now and forget all

44

about your promise. You must get an awful lot of time on your hands. You're not on duty all the time, are you?"

"Oh no! We work shifts, and get a fair amount of time off."

"And there's not much for a girl like you to find to do in Cragton, is there?"

"Hardly anything at all," Kay agreed.

"Then come and see me when you will. I never leave the house at all."

"You're very kind," Kay ventured.

"Not at all. I'm rather a selfish old woman. I keep Martin here on the estate because I can't bear to let him go elsewhere, and I know he must be very lonely here. I blackmail him to stay, although I know he would be happier away from Cameron Glen. You can see that this place is dead already, and if they flood it then that will be a fitting end to everything, but it can't happen before I die."

There was a plaintive note in the quivering old voice that touched a cord in Kay's heart, and she frowned as she studied the old lady's harsh face.

"You must find it very lonely here," Kay said.

"This has been my home all my life. I have never needed more. I live in the past, you know. There's no future for me, and the present holds no attraction whatever. I've lived too long! I ought to have died thirty years ago!"

"Life is precious! You shouldn't say such a thing!" There was horror in Kay's tones.

The old lady smiled. "I often shock Martin by talking like that, and it's become a habit. But I don't really mean anything by it. Take no notice of my wandering tongue."

Kay felt easier as she began to understand the old lady. But she looked forward anxiously to Martin's return, and when he came back into the room she was warmed by the friendly glance which he gave to her. His harsh manner had disappeared, for good, she hoped.

"Tea won't be more than a few minutes now," he announced. "I've been attending to your coat and boots, Kay." He paused and looked fully at her. "You don't mind me calling you Kay, do you?"

"Not at all." She smiled.

"Then she must call you Martin, and you must go to pick her up at the Clinic every time she wants to come and visit me," Mrs. Cameron-Boyd said chirpily.

"You two are getting friendly!" A slight frown touched his forehead for a moment. "So you're running out the red carpet for Kay, are you, Grandmother?"

"Of course! She didn't happen this way today just by mere chance, Martin. Fate has sent her to us, and I'm not going to stand idly by and let her get away again."

"I remember what happened the last time a girl came here, Grandmother."

Kay stiffened at his words, and she glanced from his face to the old lady's.

"She wasn't the right kind of girl for this place, Martin. I thought you realised that after I'd pointed out her discrepancies to you."

"Well you're not to try your hand at match-making this time, Grandmother. I won't stand for it. At the first sign of any conniving by you I shall make good my threat to go anywhere away from here, and I'll never come back."

"Your mother was a Cameron-Boyd, Martin, and you've got her blood in you." The old lady smiled thinly, and her head came up with pride. Kay, watching her closely, saw a deep glint in her old dark eyes. "You'll never be able to leave here, to turn your back upon us without another thought. You'll always be like me, tied to the place as if bound by silver chains."

"I'm not a silly old romantic like yourself!" he retorted fondly, and Kay could tell that he was only trying to tease his grandmother.

A moment or so later the maid came to tell them tea was ready, and Martin escorted

47

both of them along the hall to the afternoon room. They sat at a small table in comfortable surroundings, and the tea was wonderful. Kay expected to feel a little out of place in such palatial surroundings, but Martin sat opposite, keeping her occupied and acting as a go-between sometimes when Mrs. Cameron-Boyd flashed her eyes and put sparks into her voice. By the time the meal was at an end Kay had gained several useful impressions, and she knew she liked the old lady and felt a warm regard for Martin himself.

"Will you stay to dinner?" Mrs. Cameron-Boyd asked as they got up from the table. "It will be so nice to have your company, and Martin can quite easily drive you back to the Clinic later as sooner."

"Yes, please stay," he said quickly. "I promised to show you over the house, but I haven't had the opportunity to do so yet."

"I'll stay if you wish," Kay said, pleased with the suggestion. "Thank you for making this a very special day. I didn't expect to find such hospitality when I set out this afternoon to admire the house from a distance."

"Well that's settled." Mrs. Cameron-Boyd moved away from the table. "I'm sure you'll excuse me now, and Martin will take very good care of you. I shall lie down for an hour. It's a concession that I make to my age. But I

48

shall see you at dinner, Kay!"

Martin escorted his grandmother to the door and stood watching her depart. There was a look of tenderness on his face when he closed the door eventually and came back to Kay.

"She's a remarkable old lady, isn't she?" he demanded. "I'm so glad she's taken a liking to you. So she asked you to come and visit her at times."

"She did, and I agreed to do so."

"Good. But you will keep your promise, won't you? She'll look forward to seeing you again."

"Of course I'll keep my promise."

"You strike me as being a girl who wouldn't dream of going back on her word."

"I've never done so yet." Kay smiled as she got to her feet. "But I feel as if I've pushed my way in here, and usually I'm a most reserved person."

"It seems to me as if it was exactly the other way round!" He was smiling as he led her along the hall. "I fairly dragged you into the house, and Grandmother practically twisted your arm to get you to agree to stay and to promise to call on her again. But I would like to utter a warning here. I know what's in the back of Grandmother's mind. She's been intent upon finding me a suitable wife

49

for a great many months now. She knows what she calls suitable, and sometimes I just can't agree with her. But apart from that I am not the marrying type. I'm quite happy as I am, and I have never believed in disturbing a perfect situation. If you do come again, and I hope you will for Grandmother's sake, then be prepared to have yourself thrown at me. Grandmother obviously likes the look of you. I could see it in her eyes. She's already planning her next move. She might embarrass you sometimes with her bluntness, but if you can stick it then you should have a good time here, and help to keep her occupied. For myself, I shall pick you up at the Clinic whenever you wish to come, and I'll drive you back afterwards, but that's as far as it will go from my angle."

"Of course!" Kay spoke rather forcefully, but she felt a delicate shade of disappointment tinge her awareness. Something was happening inside her mind that she could not begin to understand. From the moment she met Martin she had subconsciously sensed that he was totally different to most of the men she had met in her life. In what way he was different she did not know, but there was an odd glow in her brain that made itself uncomfortably apparent, and she could sense unusual events preparing to shape themselves for the future. Some strange quirk of Fate had led her to this old house today, and she could imagine that Fate had not yet done with her.

"So long as you understand what will be going on here," he went on, "it won't be so awkward for you. I can understand Grandmother's point of view. She's very old now, and she would dearly love to meet the next mistress of Cameron Glen – my wife, whoever she might be."

"That's if the estate isn't flooded," Kay said slowly.

"That's the big question," he retorted bitterly.

They went on to look over the house, and Kay was enamoured with what she saw. Age showed itself everywhere, giving an intangible shade of the glories of the past in its faded gilt and furnishings. There were long corridors, dark-panelled and hung with portraits of long-dead people dressed in quaint and old-fashioned clothes, all staring sightlessly from the past as if in contemplation of the wonders of the future. If only they could arise now and see what had become of their simple way of life, Kay thought sentimentally. She liked old houses, and loved nothing better than to visit the stately homes, to wander through them and stare at their treasures. The past was so romantic! Even the musty smell of its age seemed to convey something to Kay's taut senses, and she felt reality slipping away from her as she accompanied this strange and likeable man over the many large rooms and viewed the relics of bygone ages.

"This is too marvellous for words!" she declared when they had come to the end of their viewing. "You can't let them flood this place, Martin!" She used his name without being aware of the fact, and when she looked into his face, her eyes shining with the enthusiasm that she felt, she found him watching her intently, and his features were serious.

"I'm afraid it's all out of our hands," he retorted. "I love this old place as much as Grandmother, but I'm more practical than she. I know it's no use fighting against what must be. If they decide to use this valley then my opposition would be useless. But Grandmother seems to think that I don't have my heart in the right place because I won't stand beside her with a shotgun when those men come to visit and talk."

"I can just imagine her resisting them," Kay said. "She's a splendid woman. I do hope that nothing will happen to this place."

"You've fallen in love with Cameron Glen, haven't you?"

"I've been attracted to it from the very first

glimpse," she admitted. "All winter long I've peered over this way from the Clinic, and I vowed a long time ago that I would pay a visit as soon as possible."

"It's a pity you didn't get across here sooner. It's been a very trying winter for us. You would have lightened our gloom, Kay." His tones were just audible, and she watched his face with her eyes bright and steady. She could feel her interest in him quickening, and she told herself that she had never encountered anyone so interesting in her whole life. "Grandmother seemed to wilt like a dying flower just after Christmas. I thought I was going to lose her. Everything seemed to be getting on top of her. But spring has brought her back to full awareness again, and now she's met you and taken an interest in you. That's why I'm so eager to have you visit again. You will come, won't you?"

"Of course! But you'd better tell me when to come. I wouldn't want to start pushing myself in at all inconvenient times."

"I can telephone you at the Clinic, can I?"

"Yes. We can take calls at any reasonable hour."

"Good. Then that's settled. You must let me know when you are off duty so I shan't call when you're not available. I expect being able to get away from that place at times will be a great pleasure to you, so we shan't be asking you to suffer any ordeal by coming, shall we?"

"I shall always look forward to calling," she told him softly.

They went into the library, and Kay wandered around looking at the books on the many shelves.

"This is my favourite room," Martin told her. "If you ever come to the house and can't find me, look in here. I spend most of my free time in this room."

"You have some wonderful books here," she told him.

"Do you like reading?"

"Very much." Her eyes sparkled as she held his gaze.

"Then take some books with you, in case you can't get enough reading matter at the Clinic!" Eagerness filled his tones, and Kay felt an undefinable thrill stabbing through her. It was like a physical pain, and it made her wonder for the moment about its origin.

"If I'm coming to visit here frequently then I shan't get much time for reading," she pointed out.

"Well you can spend some time reading here," he said with a smile.

Kay found that all her strangeness had fled.

She felt as if this were already her hundredth visit to Cameron Glen, instead of the first. Time seemed to have faded into obscurity, and when she glanced at her watch she failed to note the exact time. For the first time in many years she found herself completely absorbed in something other than her inner self. Her innate loneliness had been thrust aside violently by strong and determined thoughts of this man and this place. She was beginning to accept that all those months of just staring across the moors from the Clinic had been prompted by some sixth sense, some pang of clairvoyance that had projected her inner mind across the impenetrable barrier of the future to give her some idea of what lay awaiting her. Now the time had come. She had arrived, as it had probably been planned even before her birth, and she tingled as she tried to estimate just what effect all this would have upon her.

She lifted herself from her thoughts to find Martin's eyes on her, and she smiled instinctively, seeing a similar expression cross his own features. A strange longing began to infiltrate her mind. She couldn't place it as it writhed through her awareness, but she knew of its presence.

"You're a very thoughtful girl," he observed. "I don't think I've ever come across a girl as quiet as you. Are you always like this?"

"Always!" She smiled. "It's because I've always been on my own, I expect."

"But don't you ever feel the need to get out and about once in a while? You're only young once, you know!"

"I'm twenty-eight now. I expect I've got over my youthful exuberances. I've settled down. I have a responsible job, and I've made my work my whole life. I'm well set in my ways now. I don't suppose I will ever change."

He nodded slowly. "I'm something like that myself," he said. "I can understand the sense of inner peace that you must feel, but loneliness is a blight, you know. I think it's one of the worst curses of man."

She was beginning to agree with him, although she didn't admit it. There was a great deal of speculation growing in her mind, and she was powerless to prevent it. Not that she wanted to. She was too well accustomed to loneliness to want to prohibit herself the chance of making friends with fascinating people.

Mrs. Cameron-Boyd appeared again, just before dinner, and Kay never enjoyed herself more as they sat down to the meal. The ice had been thoroughly broken between them now, and they chatted as if they were old friends. Afterwards they sat and conversed on just about every topic until Mrs. Cameron-Boyd retired to her room once more. But before she went, the old lady insisted upon securing a promise from Kay to visit again, although Kay didn't need to promise. She felt that nothing would keep her from returning.

Then it was time for her to return to the Clinic, and she sat silent in Martin's car as he drove her across the lonely moorland road. Wisps of mist clung to the ground, silent and wraith-like, and Kay was glad that she hadn't walked home from her afternoon jaunt. She had the feeling that the incidents of the evening had started dramatic changes in her life, and nothing would ever seem the same again.

When she got out of the car at the Clinic, Martin lowered his window to say a few last words, and she studied his features, wanting to impress them indelibly upon her mind. But his face was already there inside her, and she knew she would never forget it. He departed after arranging to call her within a day or two, and she stood watching his departure until he was gone from sight. Only then did she heave a long sigh of regret and turn to go slowly into the Clinic. This was the end of the most wonderful day she had ever known!

FOUR

Duty next morning came a bit hard to Kay, and she was concerned as she tried to throw herself into her routine. There was so much to do that she was unable to let her personal thoughts have full sway, but she was aware that they niggled inside her while she concentrated upon her duties. Until now her whole life had been devoted to nursing, and there had never been any distraction to upset her. Now she had another interest, and she found this morning that nothing had changed from yesterday. Her feelings of elation still ran high. Her hopes were in full flood, but at the moment she had no idea what those hopes were. She only knew that she was under sudden and tremendous pressures that unsettled her and gave her great restlessness.

However the morning progressed and she gradually settled down to her duties. She made a round of the patients. There were forty-seven patients on two floors, some convalescing from illness and some recovering from operations performed at the Clinic itself. Matron came round, as was her custom, and then Robin Kent appeared for his round, and

Kay accompanied him.

Her reception of Robin Kent this morning was somewhat different, she discovered. His interest in her had never succeeded in arousing a reciprocal emotion in her, but she had felt sorry for him because he was so obviously wasting his time on her. But this morning she could arouse nothing at all for him in her heart. He greeted her as usual, and she knew his life had not changed overnight, as hers had apparently done. He kept glancing at her as they made the round, no doubt sensing some change in her manner, but she said nothing, and kept her mind on her work.

There were some patients who were more awkward and demanding than average, and these people made more fuss and caused more work than most of the other patients put together. Kay could handle them all, through her long experience, but sometimes one or another of the nurses would lose patience or fail to find enough experience to enable them to cope. This morning, as the end of the round was in sight, Kay was startled to hear a terrific crash in one of the rooms ahead, and as Robin Kent glanced at her in some astonishment, Nurse Upton came hurrying out of the room where the commotion had occurred and slammed the door.

Kay hurried forward, with Kent following quickly, and she was surprised to see Nurse Upton, a pretty brunette of twenty-four, bursting into tears.

"What on earth is wrong, Nurse?" Kay demanded sharply.

"It's Mr. Lambert, Sister," the girl said in tremulous tones, trying desperately to regain her composure. "He's just thrown his fruit juice over me, and he hurled the tray at me as I came out of the room."

Kay looked at the girl's uniform, and saw that it was soaked with orange juice. She looked into the girl's brown eyes, and saw tears there.

"All right, Nurse. You'd better slip away and change your uniform. I'll take care of this. Don't upset yourself."

The girl sighed heavily, lowered her eyes as Robin Kent came up, and hurried away along the corridor. Kay moistened her lips and turned to the door of Jeremy Lambert's room. She allowed a stern expression to sit upon her features as she opened the door and pushed it wide, looking instantly at the middle-aged man sitting up in bed with a truculent expression on his thin, pale face.

"What on earth are you doing, Mr. Lambert?" she demanded, entering the room. She paused and picked up the tray and held

60

it in one hand as she went forward to the bedside. There was a broken glass lying near the bed, and orange juice formed a sticky pool on the highly polished floor. "I thought you had more sympathy for our nurses."

"I don't like orange juice," he said doggedly, folding his arms and staring from Kay to Robin Kent, who had moved to the foot of the bed.

"You're also keen to retard your recovery, aren't you?" Kent demanded.

"I can't get out of this place quickly enough," the patient growled. He was a tall, thin and sickly man in his late forties, and he had been seriously ill for many months. He had given a lot of trouble, but Kay had always managed to handle him. But she knew by the expression on his face now that he would need a lot of humouring.

"Then stop acting like a child and let the nurses do their duty!" Kent was in no mood to be pleasant. "These girls have a difficult enough job as it is, without you making it worse. That poor nurse is in tears, and you've ruined her uniform."

"You needn't talk to me in that tone of voice," Lambert said aggressively.

"If you act like a spoiled child then you'll be treated like one," Kent said firmly. "You're not the only patient in the clinic, you know.

The nurses have more than enough to cope with. We all do everything we can to make you well, but you have to help as well, and unless you do your share then nothing we do will have any effect. Now let's take a look at you, and if you don't like orange juice then ask for something else."

Kay said nothing, seeing by Lambert's face that he was aware of the situation. She shook her head slowly as she turned to the door while Robin Kent looked at Lambert's chart and then examined the man. She looked out into the corridor and saw Nurse Strawhorn, a tall powerful Scots blonde in her middle twenties, and beckoned the girl.

"Would you clean up the mess in here, Nurse, please?" Kay said.

"I've just seen Nurse Upton," came the sharp reply in a soft brogue. "That man needs a lesson."

"I expect you could teach him one, if anyone could," Kay ventured. "But remember that he is a very sick man."

"He won't let anyone forget that," came the reply. "But you can leave him to me, Sister."

They went back into the room, and Kay found Robin Kent ready to leave. Lambert was sullen now, and refused to meet Kay's eyes. But she went to the side of his bed and spoke to him.

"It would help if you'll apologise to Nurse Upton when you see her again," she said firmly. "I'm sure she's always done her very best for you."

"I'll think about it," came the non-committal reply, and Kay left it at that.

She followed Kent out into the corridor, and he paused before they resumed their round.

"Lambert is still a very sick man, Kay," he said. "I'm not too pleased with his rate of progress. Something is holding him back. What do you know of his personal life?"

"He's married, with four children, but the children are all in their teens or twenties. As far as I know he has no worries. He's never complained to me about anything, and when I've spoken to Mrs. Lambert she's struck me as being a very sympathetic and understanding woman, very much in love with her husband. She's never mentioned any difficulties."

"Well something is bothering him. He's been with us four months now, and he ought to be in a position of going convalescent now. Have a chat with him when he's quietened down from that business. I take that as a sign that all isn't well with him. It isn't just a tantrum. He's too old and not the type for that sort of display to be natural. Try and gain his full confidence and find out what is wrong."

"I'll do that." Kay made a mental note. She sighed a little as she opened another door. "Mrs. Hall-Guthrie is still complaining about her stomach. As you know, all tests so far have been negative."

He nodded and they entered the room, where a small, grey-haired old lady was lying motionless in her bed. Her blue eyes were closed, but they opened at their entrance, and a thin smile touched the wan face as Kay and the doctor went across to the bedside.

"How are you this morning, Mrs. Hall-Guthrie?" Kent demanded. "Sister Latimer tells me you still have that pain in the stomach. Is it still in the same place?"

Kay listened while the old lady again explained her symptoms, and she watched while Kent examined her. Robin Kent was a good doctor with a fine bedside manner, and he usually managed to place his patients at ease and gain their confidence. His fleshy face always bore a smile, except when he was alone with Kay and trying to impress upon her how much he loved her. But the patients never saw that side of him, and they all liked him a great deal.

64

"I think we'll get Professor Alden to examine you the next time he comes in," Kent said to the woman. "You shouldn't be getting any pain at all now." He glanced at Kay, nodding slowly. "We'll continue with the treatment for the moment. But I want to know immediately there are any changes in her condition."

"Thank you, Doctor," Mrs. Hall-Guthrie said in gentle, refined tones. She was sixty-seven, and had never been ill in her life before. Kay automatically smoothed down the top sheet, and she smiled into the woman's face as she brushed a wisp of greying hair from the pale forehead.

"We'll soon have you up and about again, Mrs. Hall-Guthrie," she said confidently. "You're well on the way to complete recovery despite this mysterious pain."

"It could be in the mind, you know, Mrs. Hall-Guthrie," Kent said. "But whatever it is, we'll track it down and deal with it. You're not worried about it, are you?"

"I am a little concerned," the old lady said. "I was hoping to go back home now the nice weather is coming. Do you think I shall ever be able to leave this place?"

"Of course you will." Kent patted her arm. "You're doing very nicely. Just don't worry,

65

and I'm sure we'll be sending you home very soon."

They left the room and paused in the corridor. Kent looked into Kay's eyes, shaking his head slowly as he considered the patient they had just left.

"I want to go over her file again," he said. "Have those X-rays ready for me to check them, will you, Kay? I don't like that pain she's getting. She ought to be clear by now."

"I'm certain there is a complication of some sort," Kay said. "She complains of that pain most of the time, and it is rather severe sometimes."

"We'll get Professor Alden to look at her. He's due here in three days." He sighed heavily. "Kay, before we go on, I must tell you that I've never seen you looking so beautiful before, and that's saying something. There seems to be a difference about you in some way, and I just can't put my finger upon it. Your hair isn't done differently, and you're using the same shade of lipstick. What is it, can you tell me?"

Kay shook her head slowly, although she had a good idea that her experiences of the afternoon and evening before were to blame for any change in her. She guessed her eyes were sparkling more than usual, and she imagined her face was mirroring the added

66

joy that was alive and vibrant inside her. She had gained something from yesterday. A small sense of remoteness had swept itself out of her mind, and pleasure, the first beginnings of a lasting happiness, were filling the minute void that had been vacated.

"There's nothing different about me," she said brightly. "It must be your imagination."

He smiled as he shook his head, and his brown eyes were narrowed and calculating. "I don't have that kind of an imagination," he retorted. "Something has happened to you. Where did you get to yesterday? I looked for you when I returned, but no one seemed to know your whereabouts."

"I went for a walk across the moors."

"Alone? Surely you weren't out there after dark? You didn't come back here until fairly late."

"I went on into town," she said slowly, and wondered why she had lied. It would have been as simple to tell the truth. She watched his face and saw the speculation in his eyes.

"There isn't a rival for me to worry about, is there?" he demanded.

"That's a ridiculous thought!" She smiled, although she felt awkward. "We'd better get on with this round. There's so much for me to do today."

He nodded, not satisfied, and Kay considered him as they went on. She was glad that they had the patients to concern themselves about. But she knew she didn't want any more questions about her attitude of mind. She didn't know what was happening herself, and if she talked about it she might upset the fine balance of instinct that was controlling the minute changes. She knew she was changing inside, but there was nothing she could do about it. She felt that some kind of a spell had been placed upon her from the moment she drew near to Cameron Glen.

When they finished the round, Kent took her arm and tried to guide her into an empty room, but Kay put on a stern expression and pulled away from him.

"I'm on duty," she said almost angrily, and he shook his head.

"Sorry! But you're getting me into such a state that I don't know where I am. Why don't you loosen up a bit, Kay? Can't you see that I'm in love with you?"

She stared at him for long moments, her face showing something of her concern. It was out in the open at last. Before this there had been only hints and glances, and little things that didn't amount to much without thought to join them together. But now she knew for certain. He was in love with her.

She had suspected the fact, but now he had given her proof.

"Didn't you hear what I said?" He looked into her face, his eyes burning with emotion. "I'm in love with you, Kay. You're everything to me. My day begins and ends with you. I can't think of anything without you intruding into my mind. Your face is with me always. I love you!"

"Sister!" Nurse Strawhorn was calling from along the corridor, and Kay felt a sense of relief as she turned swiftly to see what was wrong. "It's Mrs. Grover, Sister. Would you come to her?"

"Kay!" He took hold of her arm as she started away from him, but she shrugged free.

"I have to go about my duty," she said in low tones.

"Let me see you later!" He followed her along the corridor. "Please let me talk to you."

"Later!" She hardly knew what she was saying. She felt panic grip her, and she didn't want any complications at this time. She wanted to run away from him, to shut the sound of his voice from her ears, but he kept at her side, and Kay knew her face was showing something of her confusion as she paused in front of Nurse Strawhorn. "What's the trouble, Nurse?" she demanded in breathless tones.

"Mrs. Grover won't take her medicine until she's spoken to you, Sister."

"We've just seen Mrs. Grover." Robin Kent's voice betrayed his impatience. "What the devil's wrong with her?"

"I'll attend to her, Doctor," Kay said softly, and he took a deep breath and sighed as he turned away.

"You know where I'll be if I should be needed," he said over his shoulder.

"You can carry on, Nurse," Kay said, and entered Mrs. Grover's room.

The patient was a youngish woman, no more than thirty-seven, tall and rather thin because of her illness, with dark hair and brown eyes. Her face was ashen, mute testimony of her illness, and she looked at Kay with a wan expression as Kay entered the room.

"What's the trouble, Mrs. Grover?" Kay demanded in solicitous tones.

"It's the medicine I have to take," the woman declared. "I can't stomach it. Do you know it makes me feel worse after I've taken it? I'm sure the doctor has made a mistake in his prescription."

"I can assure you that no mistake has been made." Kay glanced at the small tray on the bedside cabinet. "That's what Doctor Kent

70

ordered, and it's right for your illness."

"But I'm not ill!" the woman insisted urgently. "I had a nervous breakdown. That's not an illness! It could have happened to anyone, and it wasn't surprising in my case. My husband's death was quite unexpected."

"It is an illness, and you have to be treated for it," Kay insisted. "I'm sorry, Mrs. Grover, but you must drink this." She took up the tiny glass and stirred the contents. "It's got a nasty taste, I know, but it's doing you a lot of good. You'll soon be well enough to leave us, you know."

"I don't want to go out there again, Sister. I'd like to stay here for the rest of my life. There are no decisions to be made here, no worries, no strain. Everything is done for me! I never had it like that out there."

"We'll talk about that later," Kay said soothingly. "Come along and drink this, Mrs. Grover. I know it's doing you good."

The woman sighed and lifted her head, and Kay tilted the glass to her lips. She was in the lowest ebb of a depression, Kay knew, and this was what they were trying to fight. Once she overcame her depression she would stand a good chance of recovering completely.

"That's better!" Kay smiled as she set down the glass.

"I know how boring your stay here must

seem, but we're doing all we can for you, Mrs. Grover. I think the doctors have explained to you that we can only do so much. You have to make the effort to help yourself. Once you do that we can work together."

"I know you mean well, Sister! You've all been so very good to me, but you don't really know how I feel inside. It's easy for you to say obey orders and you'll get well, but I sometimes feel that I don't want to get well."

"That's all part of your illness, Mrs. Grover. That's what makes it so difficult for all of us. But you're doing all right at the moment. Just try to keep making the effort. I'll come back and see you in a little while. Try and rest now."

"Thank you!" The woman sighed heavily and closed her eyes, and Kay straightened the bedcovers and went silently from the room.

Nurse Strawhorn was waiting in the corridor. There was an expression of enquiry on her face. Kay nodded slowly.

"She's taken it, Nurse. Let me attend to her for a few days."

"She's making a hard fight of it, Sister. I can't seem to get through to her at all. I feel so sorry for her. It was bad enough for her to lose her husband like that, but to be stricken down as she is, and with a fortune in the bank, too. Do you think she will recover?"

"She will if she wants to," Kay said slowly. "That's what we have to fight, Nurse. She doesn't want to get better, and we can do nothing until she takes the first step herself."

Kay went on towards her office, having a number of reports to finish, and she wondered about Robin Kent as she sat down behind her desk. There was a conviction growing in her mind that Robin was going to make an impact upon her life. She couldn't explain it to her own satisfaction, but she was certain that he would be very troublesome now that he'd made his declaration of love, especially when she turned him down, which she would have to do without any question. She frowned as her thoughts intruded upon her work, and she looked up and stared from the window for a moment, trying to solve what seemed an insurmountable problem in her mind.

With the rounds over there was a chance of routine settling down to a steady discharge of normal duty, and Kay finished her reports and set out to check that the nurses were doing their duties correctly. She found Nurse Upton along the corridor, and paused in front of the girl, who had changed into a clean uniform and looked efficient and composed once more.

"All right now, Nurse?" she demanded.

73

"Yes, thank you, Sister. I'm sorry for that scene, but Mr. Lambert has been getting at me for a long time now. I was shocked when he threw that juice over me."

"That's all right. Don't worry about it. I gave him a good talking to, and he promised to apologise to you when next he sees you. Have you been into his room again?"

"Not yet."

"Well do so now. Change his water, or something, and I'll be on hand to see that he does apologise."

The nurse nodded and they walked along the corridor to the door of Lambert's room. Kay remained outside while the girl entered, and after a few moments, Nurse Upton emerged again, a smile on her face.

"He apologised," she said, closing the door. "Thank you, Sister. I didn't say anything to you, but he was making my life a real misery."

"You should have told me about it before," Kay said sternly. "If you can't handle a patient then let me know. Usually there is a reason for the way a patient reacts, and when a perfectly well-behaved patient suddenly starts throwing things about it's a sign that all is not going well."

"Is there a setback in Mr. Lambert's recovery then?"

"There could be! Doctor Kent isn't

satisfied with his progress. Have you any idea what could be worrying Mr. Lambert?"

"No idea at all. I have noticed the change in his manner, of course, and usually it happens when he's had a visit from one of his family."

"You're around the corridors when visitors are in the building," Kay said. "You see more of what's going on at that time than I do. Keep your eye on Mr. Lambert and his visitors, and see if you can find out if anything is bothering him. I'll have a chat with Mrs. Lambert the next time she comes. Doctor Kent wants to know what's going wrong."

"Very good, Sister." Nurse Upton went off, restored to full confidence, and Kay smiled slowly as she watched the girl's rather smart figure. She still had a lot to learn, Kay thought slowly and dragged her mind back to her work. She went back to her office to consult the diet sheets. It would be time for lunch very soon.

The matron appeared in the office doorway just after lunch, and Kay was at her desk with a pen in her hand. She didn't become aware of her superior's presence until Miss Stokes coughed slightly. Then she looked up and smiled.

"Busy, Sister?" Miss Stokes came into the office and sat down on the seat beside the desk.

"As always," Kay responded, smiling. "But that's as it should be."

"We have a patient coming in later this afternoon, and it's an emergency case. Professor Alden will be coming to operate, probably tomorrow. You will stand by to assist him, Sister. I shall get Sister Telford to stand in for you while you're in Theatre."

"Very good, Matron." Kay studied her superior's face for a moment. "What's the trouble with the patient?"

"Preliminary reports show signs of a brain tumour. It's a serious case. I shall be in Theatre with you when the operation takes place, and perhaps you'll warn Nurse Strawhorn and Nurse Vernon. We shall need all the experienced nurses we have."

"I'll attend to that, Matron. What time can we expect the patient?"

"I have his details here. Perhaps you'll put him in that room next to the theatre."

"I'll make sure it's ready for him."

"He should be arriving by ambulance between four and five." Miss Stokes got to her feet. "I understand from the telephone call that this is very serious, Sister."

"We'll do our best, Matron," Kay replied, and saw the matron nod her agreement. Her superior departed, and Kay went to check the special room beside the small, well-equipped

76

theatre. She had barely satisfied herself that the room was ready to receive a patient when Nurse Upton called her to take a telephone call, and upon entering her office she learned that the caller was Martin Searle!

FIVE

Kay felt a strange quivering in her throat as she took the telephone receiver and gave her name.

"Hello, Kay, this is Martin Searle. I'm not calling at an awkward moment, am I?"

"Not at all, Martin. It's nice to hear your voice." She wondered if she ought to have said that as she tried to control her fleeting thoughts.

"I thought I'd give you a couple of days rest from us, Kay, because we took up a lot of your time yesterday. But this is Sunday, and Grandmother has done nothing but talk about you all day. If you're off duty this evening would you care to come and spend some time with us?"

"I'd love to," she said instantly. "But I wouldn't want to appear too keen to push my way into Cameron Glen."

"I'm calling you, aren't I?" he demanded.

"That's true." She smiled as she pictured his face, and her eyes sparkled.

"What time can I call for you?"

"At about seven, I think. I shall have to hurry to get ready by then, but I won't be off duty until six today. Some afternoons I get off earlier, but this is one of the late ones."

"We'll make arrangements later about your earlier afternoons," he retorted. "All right, I'll turn up at the Clinic at about seven. Look out for me, won't you?"

"I'll be ready and waiting," she promised. "Goodbye for now, Martin."

"Goodbye, Kay."

The line went dead and she replaced the receiver, her face thoughtful, her mind working fast. She had spoken to him as if they were friends of long standing, and yet this time yesterday they hadn't even met. She caught her breath when she thought of how easy it had been for her to use his name, and he had called her by name as if he had been doing it for months. She caught her breath again as a pang struck through her. A lump rose in her throat and she felt nervous and excited.

The rest of the afternoon seemed an intolerable burden, but Kay somehow managed to live through it. Routine went on, and she was kept chasing about by the visitors who appeared in droves. But the week-ends were always hectic, and she didn't mind now she had something to look forward to. Something to look forward to! The thought stuck in her mind and would not shake loose. She was beginning to realise that she had been wasting her life. It was coming home to her now she had met Martin Searle. But how could he make all the difference? He was still a stranger, and he was only arranging for her to go to Cameron Glen because of his grandmother! Some of her exuberance faded at the thought, but she pushed it away and hurried on about her work, as if haste now would help her to get away that much earlier.

The special patient arrived at five-thirty, and Kay was more than a little surprised when she found herself watching the clock, hoping that she would be able to get the patient settled in without too much trouble. She had never watched the clock before in the whole of her career, and she felt disconcerted because she was beginning to follow the practice of the most junior of nurses. Sisters had always berated junior nurses for their habit of watching the clock, and this strange malady was coming to Kay very late in her career.

The special patient, Gordon Taylor, was unconscious when wheeled in on the stretcher, and he was put to bed immediately. Robin Kent was on hand, and carried out a preliminary examination to see how the patient had borne the long journey from the hospital. His face was grave when he looked up at Kay, who was standing by the foot of the bed. The door opened and Matron came into the room.

"How is he, Doctor?" Miss Stokes demanded.

"In a deep coma, Matron. They didn't exaggerate when they said he was seriously ill."

"Professor Alden has sent X-rays and results of tests, and they show a critical stage of illness." Miss Stokes stood looking down at the patient's immobile face. Taylor was a man about fifty. "The Professor will be here later this evening in order to maintain a watch on the patient through the night. If the patient's condition changes at all during the night the operation will take place immediately. Will you warn all Theatre personnel to stand-by, Sister?"

"Yes, Matron." Kay nodded instinctively.

"There will be a thirty-minute notice of operation, should it become necessary," Miss Stokes went on. "It means that none of those who will assist at the operation can leave the Clinic while this emergency lasts."

Kay caught her breath at the news, and thought immediately of Martin. Disappointment stole into her heart, but she kept her face expressionless. She saw Robin Kent smile.

"Well that news won't worry Kay," he said. "She never goes out. But I was going to ask her out this evening, Matron. It looks as if Fate is conspiring against me."

"I would have refused you," Kay said with a faint smile touching her lips. "It isn't only Fate against you."

Matron smiled and moved to the door. "We don't get many emergencies like this," she said. "Sister, I want a nurse in here at all times until Professor Alden arrives. I want pulse readings every thirty minutes. Any apparent change in the patient is to be reported immediately. You'll be standing by here, Doctor, won't you? Professor Alden wishes that you be here until he arrives."

"I shall be here, Matron, don't you worry. I'm interested to see what this chap is like inside."

"Well you won't get the chance to see much during the operation," Miss Stokes said with a thin smile. "You're acting as anaesthetist. You'll be too busy to see anything of the operation."

"The Professor is a surgeon in a thousand,"

81

Kent said firmly. "It's always a pleasure and a privilege to work with him."

Kay departed to detail Nurse Strawhorn to sit with the patient, and after she had given the nurse instructions she went along to her office and sat down behind the desk. She pulled a wry face as she looked up the telephone number and called Cameron Glen, and when Martin answered she had to moisten her lips before she could speak freely.

"I'm sorry, Martin," she said slowly. "But an emergency has come up and I shan't be able to leave the Clinic this evening." She told him something of the situation, and she didn't keep her disappointment from sounding in her voice.

"That's disappointing," he said instantly, "but that sort of thing is expected in your job, so we mustn't grumble about it. I'll explain to Grandmother, and we'll arrange for another evening, shall we?"

"Yes please!" She couldn't keep the eagerness out of her tones, and she heard him chuckle.

"Tomorrow evening," he said at once.

"I should be able to make that," she replied.

"Then we must wait another twenty-four hours before we can share your company." He sighed. "I hope that operation goes off all right for you tomorrow. It sounds like a dreadful job. And you work in the operating theatre, too! I didn't realise that when I was talking to you yesterday."

"I'm not just a pretty face!" Kay said lightly.

"I was aware of that as soon as I spoke to you yesterday," he told her in tones that set her heart pounding. "But my respect and admiration grows all the time. I was in hospital once. Nothing serious – appendix operation, but I saw enough of a nurse's life to respect them. I take off my hat to you, Kay."

"You're not wearing one in the house, surely," she retorted.

He laughed loudly, and Kay smiled as she imagined him at the other end of the line.

"I'll tell you what I'll do," he said. "When I hang up I'll fetch my hat, put it on, and raise it to you."

"I'd much rather you waited until I saw you again, so I could watch," she told him, and he laughed again.

"You're a tonic," he said. "No wonder they value you at the Clinic. I expect you have all your patients in stitches."

"Some of them are in stitches," she retorted gravely, and he agreed.

"Until tomorrow night then," he said. "I'm

really sorry about this evening. I know Grandmother will be upset, but I'll call you again tomorrow afternoon, shall I? At what time would it be most convenient?"

"About three. I'll be waiting for your call."

"I'll ring through on time. Goodbye now. See you tomorrow."

"Until tomorrow," she agreed, and hung up. She took a deep breath as she leaned back in her seat, and she smiled as she recalled his laughter. His voice had sounded beautiful while he had been laughing.

Kay sat thinking about him for a time, and her mind wandered as it had never done before. She felt optimistic and hopeful, and this was strange for her, unusual to an extreme, because life had always been steady and even, with hardly any highlights to disturb her. But this was a highlight, and she felt impatience race through her as she considered the many hours that stretched between her and the time when she would be able to go to Cameron Glen once more.

When she went off duty she stayed in her room, performing the many small jobs that needed doing; pressing her uniforms and taking care of her clothes and washing her hair, and all the time she thought of Martin Searle. Her mind seemed to have come alive after being dormant for most of her adult life.

She was aware now of impressions which she had never known existed before yesterday. She was inwardly agog with excitement, and her mind was having a field day with its unusual speculation and hope.

The next morning Kay went on duty prepared to assist in the Theatre. She went along to the department, and found Nurse Strawhorn already there. The Theatre was in an advanced stage of readiness, and Kay soon prepared her own part in the operation. She heard voices at the door and saw Robin Kent standing with Professor Alden. The Professor was looking in at Kay, and she smiled at him and he beckoned to her.

"Good morning, Sister!" The Professor was short and dapper, not a bit like anyone's popular conception of a very skilled medical man. He had a thick, bushy moustache that had been black but was now streaked with grey, and his blue eyes were very keen and sharp, like a hawk's, Kay imagined.

"Good morning, Professor Alden," she responded.

"I'm glad that you'll be with me on this particular case," he went on. "It's going to be very difficult. We have a problem at the moment."

Kay imagined that the case must be most difficult if it presented the Professor with any kind of a problem, but she listened intently as he continued.

"Mr. Taylor ought to have had this operation a year ago, but this illness wasn't diagnosed in time. The tumour is very close to the brain, and a complication that has arisen is a great pressure which has built up inside the skull. I've checked his eyes this morning and I'm not happy with what I saw. It seems to me as if there is tension being transmitted along the meningeal linings that cover the optic nerve to its junction point."

"Do you see this in one eye only, sir?" Kent asked with great interest.

"No, it's present in both eyes."

Kay watched both their faces as they discussed the case, and she knew a great deal of what they were saying.

"Could it be an haemorrhage, sir?" Kent asked.

"That is possible, but I don't think that's the cause, although I shan't know for certain until I've had a look inside. Of course I could easily prove it one way or another with a spinal puncture. That would tell us if there is blood. But I can't risk a release of pressure lower down because it might depress the entire brain structure. If the cause is an haemorrhage then a spinal puncture would do no harm, but if there is an oedema a lessening of the pressure would cause it to squeeze downward on the lower stem of the brain, which would bring about the swift death of the patient."

"According to all your tests, sir," Kent said, "it is a tumour. Those wave patterns indicate a lesion in the frontal-parietal area. But has the pressure in the skull lessened sufficiently for the operation to be performed this morning?"

"That is the problem. If I wait until the pressure is down, if it is going down, then I may be too late to save the patient. On the other hand, if I operate now because there is so little time left, I might kill the patient by commencing too soon. But I've already decided to wait just one more hour. Continue with the observation until ten, will you, Dr. Kent?"

"Yes, sir."

"And you'll have everything ready in Theatre, Sister?"

"Everything is ready now, Professor," Kay said instantly.

"Thank you. I'll go and have a word with Matron now. I shall be back here at ten. But call me if there is any change in the patient's condition, Doctor. One way or the other, that is. I'm sure that tumour is at the ripe stage. It could rupture at any time."

The Professor departed, and Kay looked into Robin's eyes. He seemed to lose all interest in the patient with the Professor's departure, and Kay started to turn away, to be caught by the arm and held firmly.

"I must talk to you, Kay," he said urgently.

"I still have a great deal to do, Robin," she protested, trying to disengage her arm from his hand.

"You just told the Professor that you're ready."

"I have some checking to do."

"You don't want to talk to me," he said roughly, and his tones were so harsh that she frowned as she met his gaze. "I hear that you were out on the moors on Saturday," he went on, and there was a stubborn set to his mouth. His brown eyes were narrowed, his features showing emotion. "You went to Cameron Glen, didn't you?"

"I went to look at the house, yes. I've been interested in it ever since I came."

"But what about the man who lives there? Weren't you interested in him?"

"What do you mean, Robin?"

"You know perfectly well what I mean! I'm in love with you, Kay, and you know it. I've been in love with you almost from the moment you arrived six months ago. But the minute I went off at the week-end you went

88

hiking across to the valley, and you almost threw yourself at Martin Searle! That is his name, isn't it?"

"Where have you heard all this?" Kay demanded angrily.

"I overheard Mrs. Rawdon talking to one of the housemaids. She was saying how pleased she was for your sake that you'd met this man."

"Mrs. Rawdon is rather keen on my welfare! But whatever she said, I don't see that you have any right to take that tone or that attitude with me."

"I'm in love with you!"

Kay glanced around to see if they could be overheard, and she sighed as she moved away from the doorway. Kent walked with her, still holding her arm.

"Give me a chance, Kay," he said in pleading tones. "We have been out together on the odd occasion, and I know you don't dislike me. You're such a wonderful girl. I can't sleep at night for thinking about you. Nothing else is important to me anymore. I can't settle to anything, and I'm not happy unless I can see you and talk to you."

"I'm sorry you feel like this because I can't make myself fall in love with you. I don't have any romantic feelings at all, Robin."

"That's because you've been such a lonely

girl. But if you give yourself the chance I'm sure you'll change. You need someone to take you around and cheer you up."

"I'm always pretty cheerful!"

"I didn't mean it that way. Just give me the chance to show you how I could help brighten up your life, Kay. I'm sure you won't regret it. You don't have to fall in love with me. I'd much prefer it to be a natural development. But I think you've been lonely long enough. You do need someone."

"And you think you're the man!" She looked into his eyes, but she was seeing Martin Searle, and she could feel unrest and impatience in her own breast, just as Robin had described his feelings for her, and yet he was not the object of her emotions. It was Martin!

"We've been working here together for six months," he pointed out. "We've got along well together, Kay. You know you like me. We're not strangers."

"I rather fancy that I would have discovered by now if I had any deep feelings for you, Robin," she said slowly. His face fell as he shook his head. But she cut him short and continued: "It's no use trying to bully me into going out with you. I know how I feel inside, and I don't have to think twice about it. I'm sorry I have to speak so bluntly, but you've made me do it. I'm just not the kind of girl to want romance. You'd be wasting your time on me, and I wouldn't want that. It wouldn't be right for you to raise your hopes, only to take a fall when I remain unchanged in my attitude towards you."

He looked into her face, his expression showing the true state of his feelings. She felt sorry for him, but she knew she had to be cruel to be kind. He could only suffer greater hurt if permitted to let his feelings for her grow unchecked.

"This isn't the time or the place for a discussion of this nature," he said slowly. "Let's forget it for now and talk about it later."

"I shan't be changing my mind at any time, Robin," she warned.

"You're not prepared to even give me a chance, are you? Why not? What happened this week-end to put you into such a determined mood?"

"Nothing happened this week-end," she retorted. "It's your imagination, that's all."

He stared into her face for a long, long moment, and Kay seemed to hold her breath as she watched him, only too aware of how badly he was hurt. She felt sickened as he suddenly shook his head and turned away, and she remained motionless while he strode along the corridor. His shoulders were slumped and he walked with quick, nervous strides.

There was no joy in her as she turned on her heel and went back into the theatre. She had been expecting developments from Robin for some weeks, but she wished they hadn't come so bluntly and painfully. So Mrs. Rawdon knew all about her time spent at Cameron Glen. That would be the housekeeper at Cameron Glen, no doubt. Kay considered for a moment, and then one of the nurses called to her, taking her mind from her thoughts, and she hurried across to sort out some minor detail that wasn't quite clear to her subordinate.

At ten the Professor returned to the theatre to inform Kay that the patient's condition was only slightly changed for the better.

"But I'm encouraged to think that a further delay will increase his chances, so we'll postpone for another hour," he said. "Please let your nurses take a break, Sister. It may be a long job once we start. But be ready to stand by again at short notice."

Kay thanked him and turned to dismiss the staff. She remained alone in the empty theatre, her thoughts turning slowly around the situation which seemed to be building up. But she could not agree that anything might develop between her and Martin Searle. She was a little surprised to find herself thinking along those lines, because they were still very much strangers. She tried to puzzle out why she should be thinking of Martin as a possible lover. She had never considered any man as such before, but Robin had put the idea into her head. She had to take a deep breath to try and steady her nerves as she pictured Martin's face and wondered if he would ever become interested in her.

At eleven Robin appeared, and his face was now carefully devoid of all emotion. The nurses had returned to the theatre from their break, so it was impossible for Robin to say anything of a personal nature without being overheard.

"We shan't be operating before midday," he announced. "You'd better stand down until then. The Professor thinks we shall be able to go ahead at one, but check with me at twelve, Kay."

"Yes, Doctor." She spoke politely and evenly, and she saw him wince a little at the note of formality in her tones. In that moment they both seemed to realise that nothing would ever be the same between them again, and the knowledge gave Kay a small amount of relief, because he would now begin to accept the situation as it was developing. She didn't want any complications. Her previous life had been singularly free of such emotional entanglements, and now that she had met a man who could become quite important to her she wanted nothing to go wrong with the developments.

When Robin departed again Kay took a deep breath and straightened her slim shoulders. She suddenly felt as if a door had slammed in her mind, cutting her off completely from the past and its wasted years. There was hope inside her and eagerness for the unknown. The future seemed to be promising a great deal, and she was impatient to get on and discover exactly what lay ahead of her. She could only hope that Martin Searle would play a prominent part, and now she was no longer surprised that she could link his name with her future. It seemed to fit in so perfectly . . .

SIX

Professor Alden finally decided to operate at two-thirty that afternoon. The patient showed a sudden deterioration in his condition that caused the Professor grave concern, and he hastily summoned the waiting surgical team and announced his decision. Kay approached in time to hear the Professor giving Matron and Robin Kent details of the patient.

"I'm afraid he's taken a sudden plunge for the worse," the Professor was saying. "He's had several convulsions, more pronounced on the right side."

Kay knew that meant a left-sided tumour. She took a swift breath as Kent, glancing at her, said:

"So that rules out the possibility that the patient's condition is due to an haemorrhage!"

"Absolutely." The Professor looked grave as he glanced at their intent faces. He nodded slowly. "There's still too much pressure for my liking, but this is an emergency so we have to go ahead regardless. Is the patient's family here?"

"Yes." Matron nodded. "They arrived late last night. They are with the patient now."

"I'll go and have a word with them while you get the patient ready. Let's be in Theatre as soon as possible now."

They turned away and went about their various duties, and Kay hurried into the theatre to carry out yet another check, although she knew that everything was ready. Nurse Strawhorn was busy at the sinks and checking the antiseptics. Nurse Upton was laying out the sterilised garments that would be worn by the team during the operation, and Kay went across to check that they had the small size seven wellington boots for the Professor. Then she checked her instrument trolley, and almost before she was aware of it, the rest of the team were coming into Theatre.

Matron came to Kay's side and asked for a report, and together they checked over the equipment to ensure that everything was there that might be needed. Matron's eyes were bright above her mask as she nodded her approval to Kay, and she went back to the Professor's side, where the great man was standing talking to the consultant surgeon he had brought with him to assist.

The porter looked in from the small ante-room where Robin Kent had set up the anaesthetics machine, and Kay nodded when the man caught her eye. The patient was ready to be brought in. The porter latched back the swing doors and Kay saw the patient on the trolley, with Nurse Telford and Robin Kent bending over the inert figure. Within a few moments the patient had been brought in and transferred to the operating table, which was quickly adjusted for height. They began to converge on the table, all masked and gowned and sterile. Kay pulled her trolleys into position. She would be handing the required instruments to the Professor as and when he needed them, and she took a long, deep breath to steady herself as she wiped all personal thoughts from her mind and prepared herself mentally for the ordeal that was about to begin. A craniotomy was an ordeal for all concerned, and would entail long hours of working at top pressure.

A fleeting thought touched Kay's mind as she let herself slip into the role which she had to play. Martin was going to telephone at three! She felt a sudden pang when she realised that he wouldn't be able to get her, but she consoled herself with the thought that someone would tell him she was in Theatre.

The Professor flexed his fingers in their small rubber gloves and looked around slowly to check that everything they might need was to hand. Matron was opposite Kay, ready to help, and Robin Kent was still checking the dials on his anaesthetic machine. The Professor was waiting for Kent's final report. The nurses were motionless, waiting for the operation to begin, when a stream of vital instructions would inevitably be flung at them. Silence pressed in about them, and tension grew by leaps and bounds.

Kay was watching the Professor now, seeing a glint in his eyes as he mentally prepared himself for the battle that was to come. He kept flexing his stubby fingers without realising it, and Kay had often told herself that the Professor's skilled hands looked more as if they belonged to a manual worker than to a great and noted surgeon.

"I'm all ready here, Professor," Robin Kent said suddenly, and his voice seemed to echo across the room.

"Thank you," the Professor replied, and glanced instinctively at the clock on the wall. The time was exactly two-thirty!

The patient's head had already been shaved. The operative area was just above the left ear. Kay took up some sterile towels and held them ready. She was letting her mind clear of personal thoughts, and her surgical training was coming to the fore. They began to do the preliminary work, and silence attended them as they busied themselves.

The Professor held out his hand for a scalpel, and Kay passed a gauze pad and the required instrument. As soon as the Professor had taken them Kay handed his assistant surgeon the haemostats. Her keen brown eyes watched the Professor as he began to operate. A slow, smooth movement of the scalpel in his hand opened up the patient's scalp, cutting to the bone through three-quarters of a circle, and as the incision gaped the assistant used the haemostats, seizing the cut edges and pulling the forceps to stop the bleeding. In the space of a few seconds an area the size a small saucer had been opened, exposing the pure white bone of the skull beneath.

There was deep silence in the theatre, and Kay, taking a quick, checking glance around, saw that everyone was intent about his or her business. She held out the drill that had to be used next, and the Professor glanced at her as he took it. He blinked to signify his thanks, and the next instant the faint, gruesome sound of the drill infiltrated the tense atmosphere.

The Professor worked as fast as he dared, following the line of the scalpel-cut incision. He was drilling tiny holes in the skull, and sweat began to bead his forehead as his concentration grew with his absorption. Kay stood ready with a flexible saw, and the Professor paused for a moment as he took it. Then he went to work again, cutting from one small puncture to the next, completing the circle and lifting out a circular piece of bone, to which muscles were still attached. An area of the brain lay exposed beneath.

Kay took up another scalpel and stood ready. Once again the Professor's eyes lifted to her face, but it was probable that he wasn't looking at her. He was already working against the clock with steady, speedy movements, and his brain was working out the innumerable problems that kept arising. He took the scalpel and set to work upon the tough outer covering of the brain, slitting through it to reveal the grey-white structure protected beneath. Kay saw the ominous bulge as Matron leaned forward to take a look, and the Professor uttered an unintelligible word as he viewed what lay revealed to his skilled gaze.

"It looks like a balloon," Matron ventured.

"And it's about ready to burst," the Professor added. He bent forward a little peering intently into the crater which he had cut into the patient's skull. His face above the mask was expressionless, but perspiration was beading more thickly along the lines of his brow. "We must release the pressure immediately." He looked at Kay again, and she was already taking up the instrument he was about to ask for. "Ventricle needle," he commanded, and she smiled behind her mask as she placed it in his hand. "Thank you," he said, not in appreciation for having the instrument handed to him but because of the speed with which it had been presented.

Kay watched intently. Ventricles were like chambers in the brain, and normally filled with fluid. By withdrawing the fluid the internal pressure could easily be relieved. The Professor thrust the blunt-ended instrument into the soft brain tissue, paused, then removed the stylet, and a clear fluid spurted from the open end of the needle. The tissue grew less tense as the flow continued, and the swollen surface of the brain receded. But an ominous swelling remained in the centre.

"There's the tumour," the Professor said with some satisfaction in his voice.

"I don't think I would care to try and remove it, Professor," the assistant surgeon said.

Kay watched the Professor's face. He was watching the flow of fluid from the needle, which had almost ceased now, and with a steady movement he removed the needle. He said nothing while his short, stubby, yet extra-sensitive fingers explored the area, testing and carefully probing, trying to discover the extent of the tumour. The swollen area was barely firmer than the surrounding tissue in which it nestled.

"Is it inoperable?" the assistant surgeon demanded.

"It may well be!" The Professor spoke slowly, his mind working on the questions and problems that confronted him.

Kay knew some of the questions herself, and they lay in the front of her mind. She was aware that this was a moment of great decision for the Professor. The tumour was large, and even to her eyes it appeared embedded in the brain itself. Removal might inevitably damage vital structures, and once the removal had started there could be no going back. If the tumour had penetrated deeply into the brain, and they couldn't know until it was lifted, then there would be no chance of preventing an haemorrhage.

In the vital seconds that passed, Kay could see the whole series of problems waiting to be solved, and the Professor was considering quickly, for time was not on his side. He had to use all his skill and experience to arrive at a decision, and Kay watched him while he tried to find the answers, for upon his success hung the life of their patient.

"I have no choice," the Professor said at length. "If we don't remove it, the patient may well be dead within twenty-four hours, certainly within forty-eight." He sighed heavily, and for a moment Kay could see the heavy burden of responsibility that rested squarely upon him. "We have nothing to lose. We must remove it." He looked up to stare at Robin Kent, who was seated before his machine, watching his dials intently and keeping a close check on everything.

"It's all right with me," Kent said, interpreting the Professor's glance. "He's no worse than when you started."

"He'll have to stand it," the Professor said heavily. "It's his only chance."

Silence came again and the tension seemed to increase. It clutched at Kay's throat like a ghostly hand. She watched the Professor working very carefully around the tumour to reveal it more fully. Time had long since lost all meaning. Here was a man fighting with all the skill he knew against the encroaching spectre of death that was waiting to pounce the moment he made a mistake. There was no going back. He could only go on, although he knew the odds were against him. Everyone in the team knew what was at stake and in the balance, and they were backing him to the fullest extent of their own experience and skill. Yet he was one man alone in this, and only he could ultimately win or lose the fight.

The Professor kept his hands steady as he worked. His brow was wrinkled with concentration, damp with sweat. The tumour was pinkish, a deadly fungus that had a fatal grip upon the patient's brain. He was working in a constricted space, and he knew he could not damage the growth itself and save the patient's life. The shape and colour of the tumour warned him that it was a mass of blood vessels that would very likely haemorrhage at the slightest slip of the scalpel.

He was cutting through healthy tissue very

103

close to the tumour itself, levering it aside to peer underneath, hoping to find some stalk that could be severed to free the malignant mass from the healthy brain. His concentration was taking a great toll of his nerves, although it was not apparent to anyone about him. The assistant surgeon leaned forward to get a better view, and the matron moved in closer on her side.

Kay, on her side, was watching intently as the Professor so gently lifted a part of the tumour, and she felt a spasm of horror touch her when she saw a quick welling up of blood deep within the incision. The Professor's hands stilled, for this was the most dreaded complication of brain surgery. But he did not panic, and Kay was ready with cotton pads before he held out his hands for them. He began to place the pads gently in the depths of the incision, and his insistent pressure controlled the surge of certain death.

"What happened?" his assistant asked with a quiver in his voice.

"Let me make a little dam with these pads," the Professor said, peering intently into the incision. "Now hold them in place. I'm looking for the base of this thing. I'll have to approach from the other side."

The assistant took over the small dam of pads and the Professor continued to work carefully. Kay was watching the pads for the first signs of failure. If blood soaked into them there could be no hope for the patient.

The Professor paused for a moment, but did not remove his hands from the area. He looked into Kay's face, then glanced away before returning his attention to his work. He was approaching from Kay's side of the wound now, and she could see almost as much as he. He eased up the growth, and she caught her breath when she saw a narrow stalk. This was what he had been looking for!

For a moment the Professor seemed to freeze, and then he lifted his eyes again to Kay's face. She was directly opposite him and easiest for him to see. This was a vital moment. She knew that by his face. His blue eyes seemed as sharp as chips of ice, and his pupils were contracted.

"I've found it," he said for the others, and everyone seemed to freeze as he took a scalpel and cut through the stalk. Then he lifted the growth very slowly and removed it, dropping it into a tray. It ruptured at the slight impact and blood gushed from it. Kay heaved a long sigh of relief. It had been too close for comfort.

But the Professor was already returning to the wound. He lifted the cotton pads to check for any damage that might have been caused by that ominous rush of blood. A blood vessel had been damaged by his scalpel, and he repaired it. When he stepped back a pace from the table several minutes later he heaved a long, shuddering sigh.

"Well, that's all we can do for him," he said almost jovially. "We'll close up now. How is he, Kent?"

"No noticeable change, Professor!" Robin's voice was filled with relief. "Respiration normal! Blood pressure is steady now. I think he's going to be all right."

"In a month he'll be sitting up and laughing about the way he cheated death." The Professor's eyes twinkled as he took a short moment of rest.

Kay felt herself slipping slowly down from the high pinnacle of duty. The rest would be normal now, but reaction was harsh, and she felt very tired. A glance at the clock on the wall surprised her. The time was nearly four-forty! She took a deep breath and wriggled her toes in her white boots to combat cramp. The Professor was finishing off now.

Twenty minutes later the patient was back in his bed, with a nurse watching him, and the theatre was filled with a relaxed atmosphere. Professor Alden, having thanked the team for their great co-operation, had departed with Matron and the assistant surgeon, and Kay was helping with the cleaning up. When everything had been returned to normal and the theatre floor mopped over, the nurses were dismissed and they all went off duty.

After tea, Kay's thoughts returned to Martin Searle, and she went down to telephone Cameron Glen. She was filled with anticipation while the number was being rung, and she could not believe that she was virtually in love with a stranger. She kept telling herself that he was a stranger, although he didn't seem like it. She had the feeling that they had known each other for a very long time.

"Cameron Glen. This is Martin Searle."

"Martin, this is Kay Latimer." Her heart was pounding because of the sound of his voice. "I'm so very sorry this emergency lasted as long as it did. If you rang this afternoon and couldn't get me then I do apologise."

"How did the operation go?"

"It was tricky, but barring complications the patient should be all right."

"I'm glad to hear that. I expect you're very tired now. Is it asking too much to expect you to join us this evening?"

"It would make a change to get away from here for a few hours," she said in breathless tones.

"Good. I was hoping you'd say that! Are you ready to leave now? I can be with you in ten minutes."

"Just about ready. I'll be at the door when you arrive."

"In four minutes flat. Will that do?"

"I'll be there."

"Goodbye then. See you soon." He chuckled. "I'm on my way."

The line went dead, and Kay stood for a moment, the receiver poised in her hand. She took a deep breath as she tried to recollect her scattered thoughts. Never had she felt so gay and utterly happy. Were her exalted emotions the result of knowing Martin Searle, a near stranger? It sounded like a miracle to her! Kay hurriedly replaced the phone and raced up the stairs to her quarters, knowing that she had barely three minutes in which to make her final preparations for going out. But she had taken the precaution to get ready before the call, and she was on her way down to the front door within a minute of going back into her room.

"Kay!" Robin Kent's voice stopped her in midstride as she walked along the corridor to the front door. She turned and paused, her heart lurching a little at sight of his white, tensed face.

"Not now, Robin," she said apologetically.

"I haven't much time."

His face changed still more, and Kay went on again, feeling wretched because he was miserable. He'd had as bad a day as she, and no doubt needed relaxation as much as she, but he wouldn't get it. She could imagine what he'd be doing while she was out enjoying herself. He'd be sitting in his room wondering what she was doing. She sighed as she paused at the door, and when she looked back at him she found that he was standing in the corridor staring after her. For a moment she watched him, wondering if it would help to say a few words, but she guessed that it would only make matters worse for him.

She heard a car drawing up outside, and her lips were firm as she opened the door and went out. Evening was gloomy, with a chill wind veering across the moors. There was a considerable amount of cloud, and the first stars of the evening were concealed behind the blackness that abounded in the skies. Kay recognised Martin's car, and ran to it, finding the door open for her, and she was breathless as she got in beside him.

"Hello," he said as she slammed the door. "It seems a long time since I saw you last."

"It was only two days ago. But I'm sorry about yesterday, and today, come to that. But we were standing by a long time. Professor Alden daren't operate until the last possible moment, and then he was only just in time."

"I admire you, and people like you," he said, starting the car and driving away from the Clinic. "You actually save the lives of people, don't you?"

"We have been known to accomplish that," she said with no little pride sounding in her voice. "We saved Mr. Taylor's life today."

"It must give you a wonderful sense of achievement, doing a job that's absolutely vital. You justify your existence on earth, don't you?"

"Don't you?" she countered.

"I do wonder about it sometimes," he retorted, and his teeth glinted as he smiled.

Kay watched his profile as he drove swiftly across the moors to Cameron Glen. The headlights cut a brilliant white swathe through the darkness, giving Kay the impression that they were driving along a glaring tunnel into unreality. She felt keyed up, excited, and such were the heights to which she had risen that she was unable to believe all that seemed to be happening to her. They were silent, but she was content just to sit and watch him. His face was as handsome in the gloom. His features were clear-cut, gentle. She knew instinctively the kind of man he was. He seemed to be all that she always instinctively looked for in a man.

Her pulses were racing, her heart pounding. She felt nervous and excited, and no man had ever managed to arouse her like that. And Martin was still a stranger. That much filled her with wonder.

When he drove on past Cameron Glen and kept going on the road that led eventually to town, Kay straightened in her seat and sat watching him, wondering where he was taking her. He glanced at her, a smile on his face.

"I have a confession to make," he said slowly. "Grandmother isn't expecting you this evening. She was already in bed when I came out to meet you. I used Grandmother as an excuse to get you out."

"Why?" Kay watched him intently.

"Because I wanted to take you out, after the way you interested me on Saturday," he retorted rather defensively.

"No! Why did you make up an excuse?"

"I didn't think you'd care to go out with me if I asked you point blank. So I wouldn't take the chance of being refused. I lied to you because now you're out you won't want to go back right away."

"You're using psychology now?" Kay laughed slowly. "But I am flattered, Martin.

111

I didn't realise I'd made such an impact on you."

"Well you did, and I suppose it's asking too much for you to have felt an attraction for me on the basis of a few hours of acquaintanceship, isn't it?"

"I don't know about that!" She spoke firmly, but inside she was filled with delight. This was getting better and better! She stared at his face, unable to accept immediately that he was more than a little attracted to her. But all the indications were there and she took a deep breath as she tried to control her swelling happiness.

When she had left Theatre that early evening she had been deathly tired, suffering all the reactions of the nervous and trying period they had experienced. But now she was elated beyond normal, and there was no tiredness, no tensions or worries in her. This looked like being the start of a very interesting period!

SEVEN

Martin took Kay to the largest hotel in Cragton and they sat in the lounge until it was time for a meal. Several times Martin apologised for the lack of entertainment in the town, but Kay assured him that she'd never enjoyed herself more, and she was telling the truth, she thought remotely. This was like being in heaven. The simplest pleasures were always the best, and her pleasure came this evening not from anything they could do but from the simple fact that they were together.

By the time the meal was over and they decided to leave to take a drive, Kay had gained several astonishing impressions. The most important was that her mind had opened up to Martin like a flower opening to the sunlight. She was more than ordinarily attracted to him, and an unfamiliar sensation of restlessness and anticipation gripped her as they walked out to his car. They got into the vehicle and sat for a moment.

"I've enjoyed myself," he said presently. "I don't know about you, Kay, but I like the simple pleasures. What we did tonight was just right."

"I'm on your side in this," she replied with a smile. "I don't care much for a fast pace and the bright lights."

"You've had a hard day, too," he remarked. "It's almost nine-thirty now. Do you want to go back to the Clinic yet?"

"Only if you're keen to get rid of me!"

He chuckled and started the car, and they were silent until they'd left the town behind. Kay was feeling good, although she was tired. To come out as they had done this evening was quite a treat for her, and she was aware that nothing seemed normal to her excited mind. Reality had separated from them. This was like living a fairy tale, and the more she glanced at Martin's profile the more she was certain that she'd fallen in love with him. It seemed an astonishing notion to begin with, but now she was accepting the fact, although it seemed like a miracle that had come to pass.

"Kay, I must tell you that I haven't enjoyed myself like this evening for a very long time. I've buried myself here to take care of Grandmother and run the estate. It hasn't seemed to matter before, because I love Cameron Glen as much as she. But you've turned out to be a very disturbing influence on me. It doesn't seem that we met for the first time just a few days ago. Even on Saturday I had the feeling that we'd met before, that we were not strangers. The moment I set eyes on you, before you spotted me, I knew I had to get to know you better, and that's why I was glad you had got soaked in that shower. I acted as if I had lost my temper with you because I just had to get you into the house,

114

to delay you for as long as possible. I played up the dangers that could happen to you on the moors. I want you to know that. I tricked you into staying."

"I'm very glad you did, Martin. I've been living in a rut for a very long time now, and it didn't seem to matter because I have my work, but since Saturday I've been feeling restless. I'm not satisfied with my duty and nothing else. You've unsettled me."

"That sounds very interesting." He was staring ahead, his mind on the open road and Kay half turned to face him, watching his profile with wondering eyes.

Her hands were clasped in her lap, and her fingers were trembling. She could feel a number of strange but pleasant emotions gathering in her breast, and her mind seemed to have become elevated far above normal. That a man could cause so much change inside her seemed impossible, but there was nothing else to account for this wonderful difference.

"I would warn you against Grandmother," he said slowly, after they had travelled quite some way in thoughtful silence. "If she thinks you're suitable to be the next mistress of Cameron Glen she will make your life impossible."

"She's been trying to find a wife for you?"

"She's more concerned with vetting the next mistress of the place. She would look for qualities that would fit a girl for running the house rather than concern herself with the simpler things that might suit me in a wife."

"Well she has nothing else to live for but her home," Kay said thoughtfully.

"Of course, and I humour her a great deal. But I'm just warning you that she might embarrass you with her rather blunt manner. The way she can't help talking about you now makes me think that she's already decided you're a good example of what I might need in the future. But remember that she is an old lady who has nothing but her memories to keep her going. I'd like to do what I could to help her dreams along, such as redecorating the house to bring it back to its old standard, but we don't know yet what will happen about the valley. The big decision will be made in the near future, I believe, and it's a dreadfully worrying time. I'm certain that if they decide to take our valley then the shock of it will kill Grandmother."

Kay was silent for a moment while she considered his words. Then she took a deep breath. "It's dreadful when you think about it," she ventured. "To have to move out of

116

your own home, a place that's been in your family for centuries, to make room for a reservoir is too much to expect of someone like your grandmother. The shock is very likely to kill her."

"She's very tough. She comes from very good stock, but I fear all this may be too much for her. That's why I'm glad you're going to visit her from time to time. She has lost contact with the outside world recently, and it will help her immensely to have someone like you to talk to. I'm away from the house a good deal of the time. There's quite a large estate to take care of, and I don't get much time off during the day."

"Is there something you ought to be doing now instead of having me to entertain?" she asked quietly.

"Good Lord no!" He laughed. "I have to take off some time, you know. All work and no play, as they say." He chuckled. "I did trick you this evening. But I just had to have your company. Seeing you on Saturday, then not seeing you until tonight, did something to my mind. I couldn't settle to any paperwork today. You kept appearing before my eyes, and figures fled out of my brain when you walked in."

She smiled, and he slowed the car as he glanced at her. The next moment he was pulling on to the grass verge at the side of the road, and Kay caught her breath and held it for a moment as he switched off the engine and then the headlights. He turned to her, his face shadowed now, and there was just a dim green light coming from the instrument panel.

"Kay, I don't know how you managed to slip through my guard last Saturday," he began. "I'm not even going to try to decide how it happened. All I'm concerned with right now is that you have invaded my mind and kicked me around mentally. I've never been attacked like this before in my whole life, and it's distinctly uncomfortable." He broke off for a moment and came closer as he peered into her face. "You're beautiful, you know. Those lovely dark eyes of yours! They seem to bore right through me, as if they had strange powers. They do have strange powers, because they do untold things to me when you look at me."

"I'm sorry for giving you so much trouble, especially after the way you took care of me on Saturday."

"It gave me great pleasure to see you sitting around in bare feet, and looking thoroughly at home. That's what amazes me. You walked into Cameron Glen and were immediately at home, as if you really belonged there."

118

"It's strange, but I must admit that I felt at home," Kay said softly.

He turned to her, lifting his hands to her shoulders, and Kay looked up into the blur that was his face. A car was approaching from along the road, its headlights bathing the car in pale brilliance, and she could see his face for a moment, caught the tense expression he was wearing, saw the glint of his blue eyes before the car had rushed past with such speed that its slipstream rocked their car slightly. When darkness returned behind the interruption Martin slipped his arms around her, and Kay found herself catching her breath, and emotion was piling up in her mind, staggering her with its intensity.

"May I kiss you?"

His question surprised her, and she quickly moistened her lips.

"Yes." Her voice was husky with emotion, and she closed her eyes and let go her hold upon the last of reality as he embraced her and drew her close. She tilted her face towards him and his mouth came down and touched her lips. For a moment he paused, and Kay felt a quiver start through her. Then he pulled her more closely against his chest and encircled her fully with his powerful arms. His kiss started a host of strange thrills through her. Silence pressed in about them

119

and time fled when it realised that it had lost all importance.

Kay could hardly contain her feelings. She had been kissed before by a number of men, but none had ever aroused such emotions in her. Perhaps she had built herself up for this moment. Her mind had been busy ever since she met Martin. But that hardly seemed sufficient explanation for what was happening now. There had to be other, more deeper reasons, and they were such that she could hardly begin to guess at them.

When he slowly released her he looked down at her, and Kay was breathing deeply, feeling strangely elated and thrilled.

"I've been wanting to do that ever since I first saw you," he confessed slowly, his tones set barely above a whisper. "I'm not a flirt, Kay. I hardly ever go around with a girl. I've always been too busy for that sort of thing, and it never appealed to me to play the field, as it were. But you're different. I just can't explain it. I feel as if we've been together like this for a very long time. You don't seem like a stranger to me."

She breathed deeply, letting her mind wander over her own feelings, but she was strangely unable to pick out any comment. She could only mentally agree with what he had said. She felt the same way about him, but

120

she dared not tell him.

He drew her into his arms again, kissing her tenderly, and she trembled and clutched at his shoulders as vibrant emotion tore at her. He held her tightly for long, interminable moments, and she closed her eyes and seemed to soar up into some exalted heaven of delight. When he finally released her she felt weak and shaken, and her throat was constricted and she couldn't think constructively.

"I think I'd better take you back to the Clinic," he said softly. "It's getting late, Kay. We mustn't forget that you've had a hard day."

"I shall be back on normal duty tomorrow," she replied. "I had better not be too late back there."

He sighed as he started the car. "We're not far from home," he told her as they drove on.

They were both silent on that drive, and Kay, filled as she was with so much that was wonderful and unusual, could not even imagine what to say. She felt drained of strength and will, and only her thoughts raced on unchecked as he drove the remaining miles back to the Clinic. When they arrived, Martin drove her right to the door, and they sat for a moment before she alighted.

"I suppose it's too much to ask to see you again tomorrow evening, is it?" he demanded,

121

taking her hands in his.

She trembled at their contact, and answered immediately.

"I shall be off duty at six. I can be ready by seven."

"Then I'll be here at seven." There was unconcealed joy in his tones. "Goodnight, Kay. I'll see you tomorrow."

"Goodnight, Martin, and thank you for a wonderful evening."

"The pleasure was all mine," he said firmly.

She smiled at him, and he held her hands for a moment longer, then leaned forward and kissed her lightly on the mouth. Kay got out of the car and found she was rather unsteady on her legs. He waved at her and drove slowly away, and she watched him go while her mind reeled under the vast weight of powerful impression that sought to engulf her. When he had gone she entered the building and went quickly and quietly to her room. She could not sort out anything in her mind, but she was well aware that her evening had been the most perfect she'd ever experienced.

Getting into bed, she found that although she was very tired her brain was too active to permit slumber, and she lay for a long time, reliving the wonderful events of the evening, and dwelling upon those ecstatic

122

moments when she had been in Martin's arms. She finally lapsed into slumber with her thoughts wrapped around her image of him, and she slept soundly until her small alarm clock awakened her next morning . . .

Duty came to chase away her personal thoughts, and Kay went along to her office to relieve the night nurse. Her own day staff arrived and routine began. Kay went to check the patients, greeting them and listening to complaints, but there was little change to the previous day, and she noted the more serious complaints, although most of them were frivolous, and then went to look at their special patient, Gordon Taylor. She entered the room quietly, to find Robin Kent at the bedside, and Kent's face looked as if it couldn't take on any more strain. Kay was shocked by the gaunt expression he turned on her, and she paused and looked at him for a moment. At first thought she imagined he was ill at ease because she had gone out with Martin the night before. Then she dragged her mind back to duty and glanced at the patient.

"How is he?" she whispered.

"He's been up and down all night," came the terse reply. "I haven't left him much. But I think he's going to pull through. We have to save him for the Professor!"

Kay looked at him, understanding the strain in his voice. But something else was on his mind and she knew she was the culprit.

"I saw you come in last night, Kay," he went on.

"Did you?" There was nothing she could add.

"I wish you'd let me take you out. What's this man got that I haven't?"

"I must get on," she said. "There's so much to do. Will you want a nurse to remain at the bedside this morning?"

"I don't think that will be necessary now. He recovered consciousness about an hour ago. He's in a good sleep now. But make sure someone looks at him every few minutes."

"I'll watch him myself," Kay promised. She moved to the door, wanting to get away from him, but he followed her, and was right behind when she stepped into the corridor.

"Kay! Wait a moment!" His voice was ragged. "I must talk to you!"

"Not now, please!" she begged. "I must get along."

"I won't keep you a moment. May I take you out this evening?"

"I'm sorry." She shook her head, and kept walking along the corridor, but he came after her and took hold of her arm. "Please!" Her voice was sharp. "I'm on duty, remember."

"I don't care about that." His eyes were bloodshot, and she caught the unmistakable tang of liquor on his breath. He seemed thoroughly desperate, and she set her teeth into her bottom lip as she became aware of just how badly he was suffering. "I'm at the end of my tether, Kay," he went on softly. There was a rasping note in his tones which bore out his words. "I didn't think it was possible to feel like this. What am I going to do?"

She felt guilty because she was so happy, and his misery was only too apparent. She looked into his eyes, losing herself in their intensity.

"Come along to the office and I'll get you a cup of coffee," she offered.

"Thanks." He let go of her arm and they walked along to the office in silence.

Kay rang the maid and asked for a cup of coffee to be brought to the office. She sat down at the desk and looked at her reports. There was so much to do, and yet Robin presented a problem that could not be overlooked. He was watching her, his face miserable, his eyes looking incredibly tired.

"You'd better try and get some rest, Robin," she said slowly. "You're going to crack up unless you take a grip on yourself."

"Does it show as badly as that?" He gave a thin smile, but there was no mirth in him. "Well I can blame it on the night. It was really rough. I don't think I've ever known one like it. I'm blaming you for it, because it was you in the back of my mind that kept me restless. Even when I got to bed I couldn't sleep. You kept darting across the screen of my mind. You're like a disease, Kay."

Footsteps sounded in the corridor, and Kay tensed. But Robin fell silent and remained so. The next moment Miss Stokes paused in the doorway.

"How is Mr. Taylor this morning, Doctor?" she enquired.

"I think he'll do, Matron," Robin replied wearily. He passed a hand across his eyes. "There were times last night when I thought we'd lost him, but he's rallying now. I think the worst of it is over. We should see a marked improvement in him by this evening, barring complications."

"Good. I am relieved. I'm about to ring the Professor. I'm so glad I can give him good news. Has the family rung up yet this morning, Sister?"

"I haven't taken any calls from them, Matron, but I shall tell them he's comfortable when they do ring."

"Would you say he's out of danger, Doctor?" Miss Stokes was watching Robin Kent very closely.

"I think so. I can say that with some degree of confidence, Matron. If there are no complications then we'll pull him through."

Miss Stokes thanked them and departed, and Kent heaved a long sigh. Kay shook her head slowly as she studied him, but he didn't look at her. He sat staring down at the floor, his face pensive, his lips thrust out as he brooded.

She began to work on her reports, but could not concentrate. Her mind was leaping along the even avenues of thought in her brain, but there seemed to be some side turnings in her thoughts that she had not come across before. Now she was delving into them, finding thoughts of Martin in some of them and worrying thoughts of Robin in others. She felt restless and concerned, and could only guess at the turmoil that must exist in Robin's head.

The maid arrived with a pot of coffee, and Robin took it with murmured thanks and poured himself a cup. He offered Kay a cup, but she shook her head and turned her gaze down to her work. She was going to fall behind if she didn't make an effort.

"This Martin Searle," Robin said suddenly,

127

looking up at her. "Are you interested in him, Kay?"

"He's a stranger!" she protested. "I never knew him before Saturday. How could I possibly be interested in him?"

"Strange things happen in a case like this," he retorted in darkly brooding tones. "I don't know why matters should suddenly come to a head like this. What's brought on the crisis, Kay?"

"I don't sense any crisis. It's all in your mind, Robin. I think you're overtired and overwrought. You must get some rest."

"I'm off duty tonight, I'd like nothing better than to take you out. Is it possible?"

"I'm afraid not."

"Why? Are you going out with Searle?"

"I'm going to Cameron Glen because Mrs. Cameron-Boyd asked me to visit her. Do you know her, Robin?"

"No!"

"She's a very old lady and she wants me to visit her regularly. She's very lonely, and I agreed to see her when I could."

"He's the attraction, isn't he? The grandson!"

"I told you he's a stranger, and he doesn't seem particularly keen on women, anyway."

"Then let me go with you this evening. You can introduce me as a very close friend."

128

"I couldn't do that, Robin, and you know it. I don't like the idea of pushing myself in, and I wouldn't have gone again except for the fact that Mrs. Cameron-Boyd did seem very keen to see me. It's lonely here, as you well know, and you wouldn't begrudge me an outside friend, would you? Haven't you always been telling me to get out and about more?"

"I have, but I meant out and about with me, not some stranger you can hardly trust." He spoke belligerently, and then sipped his coffee. "I wish I'd taken a more positive line with you a long time ago, Kay. But I've been a fool. I didn't want to rush you. I thought you'd fall into my arms one day, when the time was ripe. But I've been using the wrong tactics. This Searle comes along and does exactly what I avoided, and you're falling for him! My God! What a ghastly situation!"

"I'm not falling for anyone," Kay retorted almost angrily. She broke off when she heard footsteps in the corridor, and the next moment Nurse Strawhorn was looking into the office.

"Sister, it's Mrs. Grover! She wants to talk to you."

"I'll be along in a moment, Nurse!"

"She seems to be very low spirited this morning, Sister. It was all I could do to get her to speak to me. She's been sinking lower

129

and lower for days now."

"She wants a dose of gunpowder," Kent said. "There's nothing wrong with her now."

"Doctor!" Kay said warningly, and he grimaced and set down his cup.

"I'll go and have a talk with her while you get through those precious reports of yours," he said, and got to his feet and went off, almost pushing Nurse Strawhorn out of the doorway.

"Thank you, Nurse, that will be all," Kay said, and Jean Strawhorn smiled and departed.

Kay threw herself resolutely into her work and fought off her subconscious desires to slacken and think of Martin. But there was pressure in her mind, put there by Robin Kent, and she was still struggling with her thoughts when she came to the end of her reports and filed them. She left the office to carry out her official round, checking that the nurses had carried out their more routine duties, and calling their attentions to the small details which they always seemed to forget by habit but which glared at Kay as she went around.

Her whole-hearted happiness seemed to have faded since she came on duty, and she knew the reason why. Robin Kent was becoming a problem which could not be ignored. She had no idea how to handle him, and she felt responsible, in some obscure way, for the predicament in which he found himself. He was not acting, she was certain. He was really suffering because of the wonderful event which had overtaken her, although he didn't know the full extent of her involvement with Martin. But he would have to know, and soon, if his present behaviour was anything to go by, and that was where the real difficulties would begin. Of that Kay was most certain.

EIGHT

Kay had always known that some sort of divine balance operated in most lives. A little happiness was usually counter-balanced by a little worry, a pleasant surprise might come before or after a disappointment. But she had found in her life that she alternated between the medium levels of existence. She never touched the very high planes or sank down into the grim depths. She found great satisfaction in her work, and was of the nature that seemed satisfied with small blessings.

But she found herself upon a pinnacle so

high that it was breath-taking. Martin had enthralled her in such a short time that she could not recollect her scattered senses. Good sense seemed to have abated. Reality had slipped just out of touch, and she seemed to be walking on air around the Clinic, unable to quite grasp the stern reins of duty. And Robin Kent's manner gave her considerable disquiet. She was concerned about him, if only because she was a thoughtful and generous girl.

The day seemed long because she was impatient to see Martin again. Where before she never looked at the clock from one hour to the next she now found herself glancing at the minute hand and deploring its slow movement. She was becoming impatient by slow degrees, and she didn't notice it at first. The nurses became aware of her slightly changing manner, and wondered at it, and Kay tried to take a fresh grip upon herself when she realised that she was chasing her subordinates unnecessarily.

The patients seemed unnaturally troublesome today, and Kay began to wonder if there was any dramatic change in the whole of the Clinic after the months of perfect harmony. But she couldn't accept that. She had to be at fault, and she knew it.

As she hurried along to Mrs. Grover's room for the fourth time that morning, Kay tried to clear her mind of the doubts that had accumulated there around Robin Kent. It was too bad that she had to worry about her personal affairs while she was on duty. She couldn't blame Robin, but she felt that it wasn't fair that the unsuspected balance should throw up unexpected worries just when she was entering the first serious romance of her life.

Mrs. Grover was out of bed, seated in a chair by the tall window, staring listlessly through the glass at a countryside that was resting under a warming sun. Her face was pale and wan and she looked a great deal older than her thirty-seven years. She looked up at Kay again, and Kay cleared her face of all expression, although she was feeling impatient over this woman's continued calls for attention.

"What's the trouble now, Mrs. Grover?" she demanded in gently soothing tones.

"It's my head, Sister. It's aching intolerably. Do you think I could have some aspirin?"

"You had aspirin about an hour ago," Kay replied, shaking her head. "Why don't you like down and try to rest? I expect the sunlight shining in through the window has caused glare, and this would account for the headache. If you lie down I'll close the

133

curtains and darken the room."

"How do you know the sun is causing my headache? Couldn't it be another symptom of my illness?"

"I'm sure you're well advanced to total recovery, Mrs Grover. You should stop worrying about your recent illness. It's behind you now. Come and lie down, and you'll find that after a short nap your headache will be gone."

Kay went to the woman's side and took hold of her arm, helping her out of the seat. When Mrs. Grover was lying down, still complaining, she went to the windows and drew the curtains. On her way to the door she paused and spoke softly.

"Try to sleep for a bit, Mrs. Grover. I'll look in on you again presently."

The woman made no reply, and Kay went off. She glanced at her watch and went along the corridor to Gordon Taylor's room to check the man's pulse and general condition. Robin Kent had decided to have a nurse seated by the bedside again, and Nurse Upton looked up from the bedside as Kay entered the room.

"No change in his condition, Sister," the girl reported. "He's got over the shock of the operation, hasn't he?"

"All the signs are that he has," Kay

confirmed. "But he isn't completely out of the wood yet." She took the unconscious man's pulse and noted it on the chart at the foot of the bed. "I think he will soon be taking notice."

"Professor Alden is a very clever man." Nurse Upton looked into Kay's face. "I'd like to work in the theatre, Sister. Would there be a chance, do you think?"

"You will need some experience in that department," Kay told her. "If you're keen I'm sure Matron will arrange for you to take part. Of course we don't perform a great number of operations. But you ought to be able to get more than enough practice. I'll tell Matron when I see her that you are keen on surgery."

"Thank you, Sister. I've always been keen on that sort of thing. I did try to get on the theatre staff of a general hospital before I came here. I sometimes wish now that I'd succeeded."

"Why? Don't you like it here?"

"It's all right. A bit lonely, but I can't complain about that." There was a tense expression on the girl's face, and her dark eyes were narrowed, as if she were looking back into the past.

"What made you come here to this lonely place?" Kay demanded.

"Probably the same reason that most of us came here." Ann Upton pulled a wry face as she smiled slowly. "I expect we're all running away from something or we wouldn't have buried ourselves in this lonely spot."

"Well that's news to me." Kay smiled. "Are you telling me that Matron is running away from something? I wouldn't have thought that she ran away from anything in her life. And what about Sister Telford?"

"Well, she's happily married in the locality, isn't she? But Nurse Vernon isn't happy here, and yet she sticks it out. She has a family in the South of England, but they never write to her, and she doesn't write any letters."

"And what's bothering you, Nurse?" Kay looked into the girl's face. "Was it a broken romance?"

"Something like that. But that wasn't your trouble, was it, Sister? You don't look the type who would be crossed in love."

"Is that a compliment?" Kay smiled. "No I haven't been crossed in love, as you put it. But surely there are bigger fish in the sea than ever came out."

"So they say. But it's a job catching the right one."

"Are you feeling down in the dumps today for any special reason?"

"I'm usually above this sort of thing, but

today seems to be more depressive than usual. I don't know why. Perhaps it's the effect of the long winter. Now spring is creeping up on us it's like getting out of a prison, and one's fancies do tend to turn to love."

"Was it very bad for you?"

"It wasn't good. I thought I'd got over it rather well, but today proves I'm wrong in thinking so. Perhaps I need another change. Perhaps I ought to look for another position in a different part of the country."

"Is there anything I can do to help?" Kay was genuine in her demand.

"There's nothing anyone can do." Nurse Upton shook her head and returned her attention to the patient.

"Would you like me to get Nurse Strawhorn in here? If you're moving around your thoughts won't have so much opportunity to brood."

"That's all right, Sister. I'll get by."

Kay nodded and departed in thoughtful mood. It seemed that everyone had troubles of one sort or another. She frowned as she went back to her office. Was no one completely happy in this world?

The afternoon went by more quickly, and as the time when she would go off duty drew near, Kay found herself gripped by a strange impatience. She let her mind take up some of her personal thoughts, and she sat at the desk making out her reports with only half her attention upon what she was doing. She wasn't aware that Robin Kent had entered the office until he paused in front of the desk, and she was startled as she looked up at him.

"Can I talk to you when you get off duty, Kay?" His face showed that he had not managed to suppress his feelings. There was strain in every line of countenance, and his brown eyes were bleary, as if he had failed to make up on his lost sleep.

"I shall be in a hurry to get ready to go out," she replied.

"It won't take a moment for what I have to say!" His eyes glittered.

"Then why not say it now?"

"This isn't the time or the place."

"I don't see what there is to talk about, Robin. We both know what the situation is. Words won't help at all. In fact, I think the least said, the soonest mended."

"That's all it means to you!" He shook his head angrily. "I seem to be more deeply affected."

"I know that there's nothing I can do to help you." Kay kept her tones calm. "I'm only living my life as I want it to go."

"That's your answer, is it?"

"I'm not answering anything."

"You've told me there's no hope for me." He paused and glanced towards the door as footsteps sounded in the corridor. Kay studied his profile, certain that he was under very great strain, but she could do nothing to alleviate his feelings. It was not her responsibility. The fact that he was in love with her was all very flattering, but she could not accept him, and he would have to live with it. She felt great sympathy for him, but she would never be able to find love for him. That was all there was to it. She could understand that, but he would never accept it.

"Robin, you're only aggravating matters! I'd do anything to ease matters, but I'm powerless. You've got to make an effort to pull yourself together before you let yourself slide too far."

She fell silent when she saw that he was paying no heed to her words. He was watching the door, and Nurse Strawhorn appeared, her face, which was usually most composed, showing emotion akin to panic. "It's Mrs. Grover, Sister," the girl gasped. "I think she's dead!"

Robin dashed from the office, almost knocking the girl aside, and Kay got up from the desk and hurried out into the corridor. Nurse Strawhorn followed them as they went along to Mrs. Grover's room.

Kay arrived in the doorway of the room as Robin bent over the motionless figure on the bed, and she entered quietly and went to his side. He was taking Mrs. Grover's pulse, his face grave, his manner giving the impression of great seriousness.

"She's not dead!" he said at length. "But she seems to be in a coma." He lifted an eyelid. "What's she been taking?"

Kay moved forward a pace, and she trod on something hard that lay beside the bed. Bending quickly, she picked up a small aspirin bottle.

"Where did this come from?" she demanded.

Kent looked at the bottle, which was empty. "We'd better get her into Theatre," he said. "She's taken an overdose. All the signs are there."

Kay could only nod, and she was recalling her conversation with Mrs. Grover that morning. The woman had been asking for more aspirin. She'd had a headache! But where had the aspirin bottle come from?

There was no time for further consideration. Mrs. Grover was transferred to a trolley and taken into the theatre. Robin Kent seemed to lose his cloak of strain and heartbreak as he went to work, and Kay left him with Nurse Strawhorn. She went back to her office, taking the empty aspirin bottle which she found in Mrs. Grover's room. Miss Stokes was waiting in the office, and she took the aspirin bottle and studied it as if she'd never seen one before.

"Where on earth did this come from?" she demanded, and Kay shook her head. "It's got the address of the chemist in Cragton on it. Has one of the nurses bought this and given it to Mrs. Grover?"

"I'm sure no one on the staff would do such a criminal thing," Kay said firmly.

"I hope you're right." Matron looked into Kay's stern face, and her own features reflected much of the emotion that was showing in Kay. "Mrs. Grover doesn't have visitors, does she?"

"No one has ever asked to see her."

"She's told me she's all alone in the world, with her husband dead."

"Then how did the bottle come into her possession?" Kay was mystified, but she knew it was a mystery that had to be cleared up.

"Who comes into contact with her during the day?" Miss Stokes was trying to get to the heart of the matter. "Someone has done some shopping for her."

"One of the patients who is convalescent and goes into town?" Kay demanded. "But surely no one would bring in patent medicine."

"There's no telling what people will do under the impression that they are helping or being kind. There will have to be an enquiry into this, Sister."

"Of course, Matron. But it's going to be difficult to get at the truth, if Mrs. Grover won't tell us of her own free will."

"What is her condition?"

"Doctor Kent says she will be all right."

"Have you any idea how many of these tablets were taken?"

"No idea at all. The bottle holds one hundred. It might have been full, or half empty."

Miss Stokes shook her head grimly, and Kay felt a pang of apprehension as she considered the implications. Apart from the fact that she was the Sister in charge, it seemed that someone had given the tablets to Mrs. Grover, probably knowing the woman was in a depressed state. On the face of it such an action was criminal, especially if the unknown person were a nurse. But a nurse would not even consider such a dreadful action. It had to be someone else.

"I'll take this bottle with me, Sister." Miss Stokes moved to the door, and she was very perturbed as she departed, but no more so than Kay herself.

Kay went on about her duties, her thoughts with Mrs. Grover. But they had all done everything possible with the woman. Short of keeping a nurse in the same room with her, there was no chance of watching her all the time. She had advanced from her mental condition on admission to such a degree that they had been hoping to discharge her shortly. They had taken all reasonable precautions to ensure that nothing happened such as this incident, and now the worst had come to pass.

It was just before Kay was due to go off duty when Robin Kent came back into the office, and his harshly set face carried more concern than ever. He sat down in the chair beside the desk and looked into Kay's attentive face.

"How is she?" Kay demanded.

"She'll do, now," he retorted. "Get me a cup of tea, Kay, please."

She nodded and rang the kitchen. Her eyes were unmoving on his face. He looked like a stranger instead of the cheerful young man she had known and liked for the past six months. This was what emotion did to some people! But would it change her as drastically? She had no way of knowing, and began to wish for the time when this

143

period of her life would pass away. She kept telling herself that she should be happy, that this ought to have been the most wonderful phase of her whole life, but it was as if ashes were in her mouth and she could see with startling clarity that one person's actions could affect another. It was something which she had not realised before, and now she was coldly thoughtful about it.

"You don't care, do you?" He spoke harshly, jerking Kay from her thoughts, and she looked up to see his eyes upon her.

"I do care! I've been quite upset all day. But as I told you, Robin, there is nothing I can do about it."

He got to his feet and began to pace the office, and there was intensity and anger in his controlled movements. She watched him in silence, not wanting to go over the whole painful range of thoughts again. She felt hurt that he should blame her for circumstances so obviously not under her control. But she could imagine how he was suffering.

"You're going out to Cameron Glen this evening, are you?" He paused to face her again, and there was a host of powerful emotions at work in his face, each trying to gain supremacy. Kay began to wonder if he would lost control over himself, and she was a little scared as she began to divine just

144

how deeply he felt about this. But it seemed ridiculous that he should take this attitude, and she could not prevent a strand of anger from entering into her own train of thoughts.

"Robin, I don't want to hear another word about this," she said firmly. "I won't speak to you if you can't control yourself and act normally."

He glared at her, his face working, his eyes filled with powerful emotion. She heard him sigh heavily, and then he turned and walked out of the office, and Kay sat listening to his receding footsteps.

A few moments later her relief arrived, and Kay was greatly relieved to hand over duty and flee up to her quarters. She lost no time in getting out of her uniform, and her cloud of depression seemed to lift as she prepared to go out. Unreality had dogged her footsteps through the day. She had been under great mental stress, as much from her love for Martin, as from the worry that attended all thoughts of Robin. She didn't bother with tea, and at seven she was walking down to the hall in readiness for Martin's arrival.

When his car came, she left the Clinic with a great sigh of relief and hurried to where Martin was holding open the door for her. She looked into his face with avid pleasure, and sighed heavily as she got into the front seat at his side and slammed the door.

"Hello," he greeted as he drove away. "What sort of a day have you had?"

"Pretty busy, and a bit confused." She turned in her seat and glanced back at the large, square building. For the first time in six months she was utterly relieved to get away from it. A pang stabbed through her at the thought, and she couldn't help wondering what was happening to her. Did love make all this difference in a girl's life? Could it change one's principles and beliefs? She didn't like the thoughts that came crowding into her brain. She didn't like change. She had always preferred to go on in her own sweet way, but this man at her side had come into her life and started an immediate round of sweeping changes.

She looked at him as he drove the car across the moors. There was Cameron Glen before her, seeming to beckon her with its solid atmosphere. She recalled all the times she had gazed at this place from across the four miles that separated it from the Clinic. For months she'd had a strange feeling that the house would hold something of importance for her. At times she had been stirred by unknown emotions, and had wondered at her feelings. Now she seemed to understand. Martin had lived there then, and some emanation had

146

reached out across those four moorland miles and touched her awareness.

"You won't mind spending the evening at the house, will you?" he asked suddenly. "Grandmother has been asking all day about you. I told her I'd bring you over. But she'll go to bed early, so I'll be able to get you alone for a bit."

"Wasn't I supposed to come to visit your grandmother? I thought all arrangements were made with only that object in mind. But it seems as if you've stepped into the forefront and your grandmother will have to make do with what little time I can spare from the Clinic and from seeing you."

"Do you mind?" he demanded, not looking at her.

"Not in the least." She was smiling as he risked a glance in her direction.

"It's surprising, the way situations change!" he commented. "Sometimes it needs a very great effort to make any impression, and at other times it's only too simple to effect a change."

"How right you are!" She thought of Robin as she spoke, and her mind seemed to take on a coating of ice. She wished she knew how that particular situation was going to work out! She suppressed a sigh as she tried to rid her mind of the thought.

When they reached the house he parked in front of it, and they entered quickly. Kay looked around with interest, recalling her first and only visit. This house seemed so friendly towards her. She knew it was merely in her mind, but there seemed to be a welcoming atmosphere that told her a great deal. She followed Martin into a large sitting-room, and Mrs. Cameron-Boyd was seated by a large fire.

"Good evening, Mrs. Cameron-Boyd," Kay greeted, going forward to stand in front of the small figure. "And how are you keeping?"

"I'm fine, and very pleased to see you, my dear child! I thought you were going to forget your promise to an old lady, but Martin tells me you have been very busy."

"Very busy indeed," Kay said with a smile.

"Well come and sit down beside me and tell me all about your work. I'd like to hear about the places you've worked in and the people you've met. Martin, bring a chair forward for Kay. Do you think it's cold this evening, Kay, or is it just my thin blood reminding me how old I am?"

"It is extremely cold this evening," Kay agreed. "There is an illusion about the day's sunshine. The nightly temperature is still the same as ever it was."

"That's what I keep telling Martin, but he

doesn't feel the cold."

Kay sat down on the chair that Martin pulled into place for her, and she smiled at him as she caught his eye.

"Would you like a sherry, Kay?" he asked quietly.

"Yes please."

"Good. And what about you, Grandmother?"

"A glass of port for me, please, Martin."

He smiled and went across the room to a sideboard, and Kay fell to telling his grandmother about the Clinic and precisely what her duties were. An hour later she was still talking, and Mrs. Cameron-Boyd showed no signs of boredom. But when Kay finally lapsed into silence the old lady studied her for a moment, then said:

"Kay, I think you'd make a wonderful wife for Martin. He needs someone like you around."

"That's quite a compliment," Kay said, flushing a little, but she was recalling what Martin had said about his grandmother. She looked across the room at him and saw a smile on his face.

"Steady on, Grandmother," he said firmly. "Kay and I are only strangers. If you're not careful you'll scare her off, and then neither of us will ever see her again."

"Can't an old lady speak her mind?" Mrs. Cameron-Boyd demanded. "It was just passing through my thoughts, and I thought it quite right to mention it."

"I'm not embarrassed," Kay said, still smiling, and outwardly she was quite composed, but inwardly she felt on fire, and her mind had already seized upon the woman's observation and was twisting it this way and that to extract all possible significance from it. She saw the smile on Martin's face, and she nodded slowly as she caught his eye.

"You mustn't mind what I say, my dear," Mrs. Cameron-Boyd said cheerfully. "I'm just a silly old lady who can't keep her mouth closed. But I'm very happy that you've come to see me this evening, and I hope you'll come again very soon. I shall go to bed now, Martin, so make sure you see Kay home safely when she's ready to leave."

"You may be sure of that," he responded, getting to his feet. "I'll see you safely up the stairs, Grandmother! Kay will come to see you again, I promise."

"I know she will," the old lady retorted decisively. "I knew from the moment I saw her that she would become a regular visitor here."

She smiled at Kay as Martin took her arm and led her out of the room, and Kay sat quite still, filled with wonder, until Martin returned. There seemed to be some intangible power at work here! Of that Kay was sure, but she couldn't begin to understand what it was all about. The only thing she could do was wait and see what transpired . . .

NINE

Sitting alone with Martin afterwards, Kay found herself relaxing for the very first time that day, and she sighed and leaned against him as he slipped an arm about her slim shoulders.

"You're looking tired and tense, Kay," he remarked.

"It has been rather hectic."

She was thinking of Robin Kent and not her work as she spoke, but Martin naturally imagined that she meant the Clinic.

"Do they work you so hard all the time?"

"It isn't so much the work as the surrounding connections. I love my work, but I think there are too many side issues at the moment."

"Not connected with the Clinic?" His eyes were steady as he studied her, and Kay looked into his face, still thinking of Robin Kent.

"I do have some personal problems," she

began cautiously.

"Like to tell me about them?" He drew her closer, his arm tightening around her.

Kay felt a great desire to talk about Robin, feeling that perhaps a discussion of the problem might lead to a solution turning up. But she didn't think she could talk about it to Martin, and the fact that his steady eyes watched her intently all the time did much to dissuade her against opening up her heart.

"Is it too personal?" he pressed.

"Not really." She drew a sharp breath.

"I'm sorry." He turned to her and took her into his arms. "I don't want to pry, Kay, but unless I'm very much mistaken you're under a great deal of pressure – more than is good for you. I know how hard you have to work, and you don't need all that many problems to make life well nigh impossible. If there is anything I can help with then don't hesitate to tell me."

"Thank you for the offer!" She smiled, trying to convey by her manner that all was well. "You're a very thoughtful man, Martin. But there's nothing so serious as to warrant a full scale enquiry."

"I'm glad to hear it. I won't question you further." He kissed her lightly, and Kay clutched at him, filled with sudden emotion.

She closed her eyes and felt her mind slowly drain of all mundane thoughts. If only he could have done this earlier, she found herself thinking. He had the power to wipe her mind clean of trouble.

She opened her eyes as he released her, and found him watching her intently. There was still a questioning light in his blue eyes, and she knew by his expression that she had failed to convince him that nothing was wrong.

"We have had some trouble at the Clinic," she said. "One of our patients is recovering from a nervous breakdown. Her husband was killed in an accident and she took it so very badly. She somehow got hold of a bottle of aspirin, and took an overdose today."

"Is she dead?"

"No. Fortunately we got to her in time, but there's to be an enquiry into how she managed to get the aspirin."

"Will this affect you at all?" He held her gently by the shoulders.

"I was the Sister on duty, of course, but that's not what's worrying me! Where did she get the aspirin from?"

"Have you tried the process of elimination?" he enquired.

"I don't think that would work. There are so many people she might have come into contact with, apart from the nursing staff.

153

Some of our patients are merely convalescent. They come and go freely during the day. Any one of them could have bought the tablets for her. They were in a bottle labelled by some chemist in Cragton."

"Well it is a problem!" He nodded slowly as he watched her face. "Poor Kay! It certainly would account for your uneasiness. But try and forget it for this evening. I'm sure the truth will come out." He paused as a thought seemed to strike him. "You couldn't lose your job through this, could you?"

"It didn't occur through negligence on my part, and I don't have to search the patients to ensure they have nothing in their possession that would retard their recovery." Kay took a deep breath and sighed. "No, I don't think it will affect me in that way. But what does concern me is that whoever has bought the tablets, for whatever reason, may do so again for another patient. Anything could happen."

"So I can imagine." He gathered her into his arms again and kissed her passionately. "Come along, my love, try and forget all this for now. You can't help matters by brooding over it. Let me try and cheer you up for an hour or so."

She smiled, and didn't tell him that the business with Mrs. Grover was only half the trouble. She found thoughts of Robin Kent slipping through her defences and wreaking havoc in her mind. If only she knew how to help him! She sighed again, and Martin leaned away from her, shaking his head slowly.

"I can't do anything to help you," he said. "I just can't get through to you, Kay."

"I'm sorry. I'm afraid that I'm not very good company this evening."

"Don't worry about me. Let's try and do something about you. Shall we go for a drive?"

"I'd much rather sit here and just chat."

"So would I." He smiled. "I just thought it might help to take your mind off things."

She studied his intent face for a moment, seeing the concern in his eyes, and she had to tell herself that they hadn't known each other a complete week yet! It seemed fantastic that they could have come so close in such a short time.

"What are you thinking now?" he demanded gently.

"I was just telling myself that we've known each other only a few days, and yet here we are like friends of long standing. How do you account for it?"

"I wouldn't dream of trying to account for it. A strange power has been at work on us, Kay, I do believe, and I certainly wouldn't question it. I can't believe it myself, you know. When I look at you and see how much you've slipped into my thoughts and my life I can only marvel. This time last week we didn't know each other existed, and now you know that I care a great deal about you and I know you have feelings for me."

"Some people go through an entire lifetime without meeting the important person, the one who means more to them than anyone else ever could!" Kay nodded slowly.

"And you think I'm the important person in your life?"

"I'm sure of it," she replied.

He gathered her into his arms again, and Kay felt her worries slipping away. It was good to feel his arms about her, to know that he did care for her. She didn't have to don a thinking cap in order to discover what he meant to her. There was a tiny voice in the back of her mind, insistent and powerful, telling her repeatedly that he was the one. The feel of his arms about her, the touch of his lips, told her the same tale. They were meant for each other.

Time slipped away from them like an ebbing tide, and Kay found her mind clearing for the first time that day. Even her worries about Robin Kent slipped into perspective for a time and she knew complete contentment. But time passed despite the fact they were not aware of it. The clock on the big mantelpiece chimed musically and Kay counted the strokes, tensing when she reached ten.

"It's time to call it a day, I suppose," Martin said, releasing her with a sigh. "I can't account for it, but the days seem to last a lifetime now, and the evenings with you are over in a flash. There's something wrong somewhere."

"I've just begun to notice the same thing," she told him.

"Have you ever been in love before, Kay?" He looked intent as he watched her face.

"Not in love," she said with a sigh. "I've had a boyfriend or two, but it's never been anything serious."

"That's what I thought." He paused. "I did know a girl once who had become a bit special. But she went off with another fellow while I was at college. I haven't looked at a girl since." He smiled. "Don't think I've been grieving for a lost love, or anything like that. I've always been too busy to think of girls. I do know several girls in this area. One can't help meeting them at various functions. But there's never been anyone else in my heart, Kay, until I met you."

"How can you be so sure that I am important?" she asked softly. "It doesn't seem possible, does it?"

"Am I important to you?" he countered.

"Yes." She had to moisten her lips before she could speak.

"And how do you know that I'm important to you?"

"I don't know for certain." She shook her head and smiled. "I'm getting confused, aren't I? What I mean is, I know subconsciously that you're important. It isn't something that has to come to the forefront of my mind."

"You don't have to convince me," he retorted. "I'm just trying to get you to illustrate exactly how I know about you."

"And do you get the same reaction as me?"

"Near enough!" He nodded and took her into his arms, his face showing tenderness. "It is as I suspected. We do feel the same way about one another. But I'm not going to confuse the issues by talking about love and Fate and all that sort of thing. I've never been an impatient man, Kay, but you're pushing me into a great many emotions that I never knew existed. However I've got to give the both of us time to think."

Her eyes were bright as she smiled. She felt about the same intensity of emotion that held him. It seemed uncanny to her that they should meet and come together so simply and easily, after so many years of having no romance at all. It seemed to Kay that Fate had indeed taken a hand in their lives, as if they had been destined for each other from the very moment that time began. It seemed such a short time to them, but in the course of eternity; from its very start when all fates were decided instantly by some omniscient being, it was merely the unfolding of the first important chapter of their lives. They had been kept apart until the right moment, and now that they'd met their special influences were busy tying up their former loose ends. Their destinies had become entwined, and they would never be able to go forward alone ever again.

She felt a strange sense of security as he stood up and drew her upright. His hands upon her shoulders were heavy, yet caressing, and she felt reluctant to go back to the Clinic and the worries which she knew awaited her there. Reality was harsh. It was lying in wait for her outside this big old house that had proved such a haven. He kissed her, and she felt herself sagging in his arms as if her very strength was being sapped by the power of his ardour.

"Kay, I'm so very glad that I met you," he whispered. "I've never known a girl like you before. I'm glad that something made me wait for you to come along."

"We must take time," she warned. "We must make certain that these are true feelings which we feel."

"I'm already certain about myself, but you take as much time as you need, my dearest," he whispered.

"I'm certain, as far as it goes." Something seemed to fill her with reluctance, and she imagined that she was afraid a calamity would occur which would rob them of each other. So many things could happen, and at this blithe moment she could not consider losing him. All her hopes were directed towards him. The empty years seemed to have faded with the onset of this love that gripped her. What happened before they met seemed to have faded into oblivion, and all that had occurred since seemed like a wonderful dream. And she was so very afraid of coming to a grim awakening, to find it had been nothing but a dream.

"Come along!" He spoke sharply, dispelling some of the unreality that surrounded them. "It's getting very late, Kay, and I know you have to be up early in the morning."

She smiled at his thoughtfulness, and tilted her face for another kiss. He held her close, exerting all his strength for a moment, and she was crushed against him, laughing, elated by the feelings which were aroused inside. Then he stepped away and sighed, taking her hand to lead her from the room. They fetched her coat and went out to the cold, dark night, hurrying to the car and getting inside.

Kay felt breathless as he drove back across the moors. She leaned back in her seat and lazily watched the road ahead unfolding in the headlights. This was becoming familiar territory. She thought of the times she had come along this road during the winter, before she had known him, and she wished they could have met a lot earlier in life. From time to time she glanced at him. His face was set, intent as he concentrated upon his driving. It was a handsome face, ruggedly attractive, and the shape of it, the angles of the forehead and jaw, fitted into her mental picture of her dream man. She had always wanted someone just like him!

All too soon they reached the Clinic, and Martin dipped the lights as he drove slowly towards the house. Kay stopped him before he reached the door.

"It's getting late," she pointed out, and he stopped instantly. "If we wake up some of the patients they'll have a difficult job getting back to sleep."

"That thought crossed my mind last

evening," he said. "I'm glad to see that you're so very thoughtful and considerate."

"That consists of most of my work," she replied.

"I'll walk up to the house with you." He started to get out of the car, but she put a hand on his arm and stopped him.

"No. I'll go on alone. It isn't far. You haven't got an overcoat on and it's cold out there tonight."

"I'll be all right," he insisted. "It's dark up to the house."

"I've walked it many times," she retorted with a smile.

"But that was before you met me!"

She pushed her way into his arms and her lips stopped the rest of what he was going to say. He kissed her eagerly, and Kay felt uplifted far above the normal plane. She was breathless when she eased back from him.

"When shall I see you again?" she asked softly.

"Tomorrow evening?" he said eagerly.

"I shall have to stay in some nights each week."

"We've all the working days to be apart," he said. "I want to see you as often as possible. I've just got to know if this is true love or not, and the only way I'll find out is by seeing you every day for six months."

She smiled and began to get out of the car. "All right," she said. "I'll see you tomorrow evening, if you wish. At what time shall I expect you?"

"About three in the afternoon?" he suggested with a smile.

"Make it seven in the evening and I can be ready," she replied with a chuckle.

"Don't you ever get any afternoons off duty?"

"Yes. I shall be finishing at one on Thursday. And I have all Friday off."

"Why didn't you tell me this before?" He seized her hand. "I could have made some arrangements for taking you out for the day. Would you like that?"

"Nothing would please me more," she said.

"We'll go out Thursday afternoon and evening, and again all day on Friday. But I expect you'll be sick of the sight of me by the time Saturday comes."

"I doubt it, but we'll give it a trial, shall we?"

"You bet we will!" He kissed her again, and Kay clung to him as if her very life depended upon their closeness.

But eventually she drew away from him and got out of the car. She looked down into his face before closing the door. He smiled up at her, his face in shadows, but she could see his appeal quite plainly, and she took that picture of him into her mind and placed it upon a pedestal.

"Goodnight, my dearest," he said softly.

"Goodnight, Martin. See you tomorrow night!" She took a last lingering look at him and then closed the car door. She stepped back and watched him turn the vehicle, and he waved to her as he departed. Kay stood motionless until he had gone, and then she sighed heavily and turned to face the house. She was standing in darkness, but she could see the way clearly because a number of large windows gave ample light to the surrounding grounds. She put her hands into her pockets and hunched her shoulders a little as she walked up the drive. All the events of the evening were fixed very firmly in her mind.

Kay stepped on the grass to muffle the sound of her feet, and she passed under some trees that were grouped just before the house. Her mind was not on her surroundings. Her thoughts were filled with Martin. When a black shadow moved slightly on her left she paused instantly, feeling startled, dragged as she was from her thoughts. Then she caught her breath and took a grip on her nerves. It was probably one of the off-duty nurses saying goodnight to a local boyfriend, she thought with a smile. But when she went on again the figure moved, and suddenly came towards her.

She halted, a little shocked for no apparent reason. She had seen figures in the grounds before when she'd been returning from town. But usually there were two figures together, and this one was obviously making towards her. She began to feel nervous, and had started to back away when her name was called in a vibrant whisper.

"Kay, is that you?"

She frowned as she halted, for it sounded like Robin Kent, and a little spurt of anger found its way into her mind because he had startled her.

"Robin, what on earth are you doing out here?"

"I've got to talk to you, Kay. I knew you were still out, and I've just done a round of the patients. I've got a little time to spare."

"But I haven't, Robin, and this is no place to be standing at this time of night. Supposing someone else had been coming along here instead of me? You wouldn't have had a plausible excuse for being out here. That's the way to start talk going around, you know."

"I don't care about anything but you," he said fiercely. "I must talk to you. I shall go mad if I don't get something settled."

Kay suppressed a shiver. The night was

165

cold, despite the sunshine of the day. She knew nothing would be solved by talking. He was the only one who could do anything about the situation, but she knew he wouldn't accept the only way out, which was to forget about her.

"I must go in," she said slowly. "It's late, and I'm cold, Robin."

"You haven't worried about the time until now, have you?"

"I don't think that's any of your business. Look, I feel sorry about this. I didn't know you were in love with me. But it would not have made any difference if I had known. I'm not in love with you, Robin." She sighed. "We've been over all this before. We're just wasting time."

"It may seem like wasting time to you, but I'm in the last stages of despair, Kay. I couldn't sleep last night, and it's going to be just as bad tonight."

"What can I do to help you?" she demanded. "But I can't fall in love with you to order."

"I know that!" His tones were rasping. "All I ask is that you give me some hope, Kay. Anything would do to cling to."

"I can't do that." She shook her head slowly, clenching her hands as a cold shiver ran down her spine.

166

"So you've gone and fallen for that other chap!" He spoke through his teeth, and then he reached out and seized hold of Kay's wrist in a powerful grip. His strength gained from his frustration, and she cried out at the pain in her arm.

"Please let me go," she said quickly, furiously. "This won't help at all."

"Perhaps not, but it may release some of the pent up feelings tormenting me." He pulled her almost brutally into his grip and embraced her, pressing his face against hers.

Kay struggled against him, sickened a little by the smell of liquor on his breath, but she could not get away from him, and he began to kiss her, passionately and violently. She was almost suffocated by his desire. But there was a disturbance behind them that startled Kent as well as Kay. A torch was switched on and a voice demanded their identities. Kay felt a swift surging of panic, for she recognised Matron's voice!

TEN

Silence followed the curt demand for identity, and Kent released Kay as if she had suddenly become too hot to hold. Kay looked into the beam of the torch and was momentarily blinded. She looked away, felt Kent move back from her, and then the light went out. Kay still could not see, but she heard Matron's voice.

"This is not the place for an assignation, Sister."

By the time Kay could begin to see details again she discovered that Matron had moved on, and her cheeks burned as she imagined what her superior must be thinking. She turned on Kent, who was standing silent at her side, his passion spent or startled out of him, and she felt anger begin to rise.

"What on earth is Miss Stokes thinking at this moment?" she gasped.

"It doesn't matter what she thinks. You're not breaking any rules out here. You're not on duty."

"That's beside the point. I wasn't breaking any rules! I didn't do anything. This is the limit, Robin. I shall never speak to you again if you persist in this behaviour. For the last time I'm telling you to pull yourself together. The Lord knows what Matron must be thinking."

"It's none of her business! Kay, can't you see what you're doing to me?"

"I'm not doing anything. You're doing it to

yourself, Robin. Try and snap out of it before you do something you'll be really sorry for. You know this can't go on."

He made no reply, and Kay suppressed a shiver. She felt unclean because of the imprint of his drink-laden breath against her cheek, the pressure she could still feel where he had kissed her.

"I'm going in," she said slowly. "Goodnight."

He made no move to prevent her leaving, and Kay hurried away and entered the big house. She was breathless, angry and embarrassed, and she didn't know how she would manage to face Miss Stokes again. She felt that she would have to explain to her superior exactly what had happened, but any explanation might make the whole thing seem more important than it really was.

Going up to her room, she hurriedly undressed and slipped into her dressing gown. Snatching up her towel she went along to the bathroom and scrubbed her face with as much violence as she could stand. She felt better when she went back to her room, but sleep would not come immediately, and she was disappointed to discover that all those wonderful impressions of the evening with Martin had been chased into the background and destroyed by Robin's bad behaviour.

Eventually she slept, but badly, and several times she almost came back to consciousness. She was aware of every turn she made, and in the morning, when she finally opened her eyes to greet the new day, she was very reluctant to get out of bed and begin her routine. She didn't want to set eyes on Matron ever again. Her cheeks turned scarlet at the thought. And as for Robin himself! She suppressed an indignant sigh and made the effort to get up. She felt as if she hadn't slept a wink all night!

Going on duty, Kay found herself filled with a strange attitude. Already she was looking forward to going off duty. Even the thought that next day she had the afternoon off, and the day free on Friday, did not make much impression. Wednesday was before her and it promised to be troublesome . . .

She was pleased to find a marked improvement in the condition of Gordon Taylor. He had regained full consciousness the evening before, although he was asleep when Kay looked in on him. The chart gave her enough information to know that he was doing very well.

On her round, she entered Mrs. Grover's room, to find the woman propped up in her bed, wan and very depressed. Going to the foot of the bed, Kay looked down at her patient.

"How are you feeling this morning, Mrs. Grover?" she demanded.

For a moment there was no reply. The woman was staring fixedly at the opposite wall, and the sound of Kay's voice seemed to strike her physically. She tremored a little, then stirred and sighed. When she looked into Kay's face there was no animation in her eyes. Kay had never seen such appeal in human eyes before. The woman badly needed help, and of the kind that Kay was not qualified to give.

"I'm as well as can be expected, Sister!" Mrs. Grover said slowly. Her voice was pitched low, her tones dead, expressionless.

"Has Matron, or anyone spoken to you about this –!" Kay paused for a moment before adding – "incident?"

"You'll be wasting your time if you do ask," came the swift reply.

"This is a very serious business." Kay knew she ought to leave the questioning to Matron, but she wanted to know if one of the nurses was to blame for the lapse of duty.

"It's my life, isn't it? If I choose to end it then why should you worry?"

"You don't expect me to answer that question, surely." Kay shook her head.

"You've been doing so wonderfully well, Mrs. Grover. You're still young. You could make a good life for yourself. Why don't you give yourself the chance that you deserve?"

"You're only concerned about my health. You want to make me well and then pitch me out into the world again. That's all you know about it, isn't it?"

"I know that you've got to make a fight to regain your mental balance, that at the moment you are filled with morbid pain that can't be eased by any medicine. I know time is your greatest enemy, that your memories hurt you every waking moment of your life." Kay spoke vibrantly, her voice pitched little above a whisper. "I think I understand perfectly the kind of hell you're living. I can't know the degree of your pain, but I know you're suffering. But you owe it to the memory of your husband to live and enjoy life. You think of him every moment, don't you?"

"Every moment," Mrs. Grover echoed.

"And if he were still alive you would want to do what pleased him, wouldn't you?"

"Of course."

"What would he think of you now, if he could know about all this?" Kay looked into the woman's dark eyes, holding her attention. "Would he be pleased to know that you're

throwing away your life? Wasn't life precious
to him?"

"It was precious to me while he was alive.
Now he's gone there is nothing to live for."
It was a cry straight from the woman's heart,
and Kay winced a little inside, but she knew
she could not let up.

"Your husband worked hard for you while
he was alive, didn't he? You're well provided
for."

"What's that got to do with it?"

"Nothing, only that he did his utmost to
give you everything. That must have been his
dearest wish while he was alive. So why aren't
you doing everything you can to enjoy what
he left you? It is what he would want, isn't
it?"

Mrs. Grover did not answer, but a
thoughtful expression had come into her
face. Kay noticed the door opening slightly,
and she saw Matron standing there, listening,
and Miss Stokes remained outside.

"It is right that one should show and feel
grief for the loss of a loved one," Kay went
on. "But grief is a selfish emotion too. Did
you know that? It is a great emotion for
wallowing in. But that's the easy way out.
It takes determination and faith to face up to
facts and go on living when everything seems
hopeless. But open your mind, Mrs. Grover,

to the fact that your husband loved life and would wish you to go on living. Do what he would have wanted you to. Start living again. Get yourself out of here and go back to the world. Let everyone who knows you see that you loved your husband enough to go on living for him."

Mrs. Grover burst into tears and put her hands to her face. Kay felt tears come to her eyes, and she went to the woman's side and gently patted her shoulder.

"Your tears will help," she said softly. "But don't think you are all alone in the world. If you look around you'll find a lot of people in much worse plight than yourself. Try to look outward and you'll do all right. It won't be easy at first, but you'll make it. You're the kind of woman who can pull out enough to win."

Mrs. Grover said nothing, and Kay stroked the woman's dark hair, then departed softly, closing the door gently. Miss Stokes was waiting in the corridor, and Kay was so involved with emotion that she did not feel awkward about the incident which Matron had witnessed the night before in the driveway.

"I'm glad I overheard what you said to Mrs. Grover," Miss Stokes said. "I was intending to give her a talk on the same lines, but you

174

did it admirably. I would leave her to her thoughts for a time now. But don't leave her too long. Keep looking in on her. Say nothing more to her unless she begins to talk to you about it first."

"I'll watch her closely," Kay promised. "Poor woman! She is so near to complete recovery, and so far."

"I'll have her see a psychiatrist in a day or two. Mr. Fleming is coming in next Tuesday. We'll arrange for him to see her. Did you question her about the aspirins?"

"I taxed her but she wouldn't say, and I think it's best to let the matter drop, Matron."

"I certainly wouldn't dream of cross-examining her." Miss Stokes smiled, but there was a seriousness in her expression which Kay could not miss. "I am concerned in case one of the staff is involved."

"I wouldn't believe that under any circumstances," Kay said.

"I'd hate to think it might be the true state of affairs. I couldn't believe one of our nurses would deliberately do such a thing, knowing the state of Mrs. Grover's mind."

"Then it has to be one of the patients who has been into town."

Miss Stokes nodded slowly. "I can quite easily check on them. There are only half a dozen patients who come into that category. Have you seen anyone making friends with Mrs. Grover?"

"Several patients have been taking notice of her because we asked them to. It's all part of Mrs. Grover's treatment."

"Well I'll check up on that angle as soon as I can. There's no telling where this sort of thing might lead to. It has got to be stopped, Sister."

"I agree, Matron."

Miss Stokes nodded and turned away, and Kay thought of what had happened the previous night.

"Matron," she said, and hesitated as the woman turned to face her. Kay began to colour slightly. "About last night," she said awkwardly. "I feel an explanation ought to be made."

"Say nothing, Sister." A smile touched Miss Stokes' lips. "It's none of my business. You were off duty, although Doctor Kent was on call. But then he's always on call, being the only resident doctor. I'm sorry I interrupted you. It was none of my business, but I saw your figures and didn't know who was there."

"That isn't the point, Matron." Kay paused, knowing she could not tell what really happened. It would put Robin in a poor light. The least said, she thought remotely, and shook her head. "Very well," she said.

"Carry on, Sister," Miss Stokes said, smiling, and she went on her way.

Kay felt a little better after that, and the morning seemed to move with a faster tempo. From time to time she looked in upon Mrs. Grover, and found the woman quiet and contemplative. But she was really waiting for Robin to appear to make his round, and he did finally turn up almost half an hour late. When he came into the doorway of her office, Kay was seated at the desk writing up her morning reports. She looked up and found him staring at her, and she was shocked by his ghastly expression. He looked as if he hadn't slept for a week, and his eyes were bloodshot and staring. She sensed that he had been drinking, and hoped that no one else would notice his condition.

"You'd better come in and sit down for a moment," she advised. "Would you like some black coffee?"

He nodded silently and came to take his customary seat, and Kay rang the kitchen, asking for a pot of coffee. She watched his face for a moment, wondering at the thoughts passing through his mind. He seemed like a stranger, more of a stranger to her than Martin! He looked up at her, silently regarding her with an air of sullen reluctance. He didn't want to maintain his friendliness with her and yet he could not keep a barrier between them. She felt pity for him, but knew it was a helpless emotion when all he wanted was her love.

"I suppose I'd better start looking for another position," he said at length.

"You're leaving here?" There was surprise in Kay's tones.

"What else can I do? You're not leaving, and we both can't stay here."

She regarded him in silence for some moments. Her thoughts seemed to have halted, and for the space of several heartbeats she could not get even her imagination to work. Then she drew a deep breath and exhaled sharply.

"Are you trying to put more pressure on me, Robin?" she asked.

"The pressure is on me!" He glared at her. "I don't think you realise just how badly you're affecting me. This isn't just some game I'm playing. I can't help myself, and I'm putting my whole career in jeopardy. I love you, Kay, and nothing will ever change that."

She watched him intently, trying to look through his appearance and manner, hoping to catch a glimpse of what was really passing through his mind. But he didn't seem to have

178

a clear idea himself of what he wanted. He was halfway between two points. His passion for her was goading him into an unnatural frame of mind, and this was aggravating him, making him worse, causing him to suffer more. Her sympathy was aroused. She felt sorry for him. But it wasn't helping him in any way.

"You've got nothing to say," he rebuked. "You don't care how I feel."

"I do care, but there's nothing I can do about it," she retorted. "How can I help? Tell me that."

"Give me a chance to love you!"

"That's impossible, Robin, and you know it. Even if I were fool enough to try, how much success do you think we'd have? I'm not in love with you and no pressure from any quarter can make it any different."

He stared at her, and a tense silence followed. Then a maid arrived with a tray, and Kay poured his coffee for him. He sat sipping it in silence, and Kay watched his tense face, noting the pallor in his cheeks, the restrained emotion in his eyes, and the more obvious signs of his faltering determination. When he sighed for the second time in quick succession Kay moistened her lips.

"You've got it bad, Robin," she said.

"There's only one cure and you've suggested that."

"Me finding another position!" A thin smile flitted across his lips. "I know the cure all right. I'm a doctor. So I'll have to get out. How long do you think it will take me to get over you?"

She shrugged, not wanting to prolong the agony. But he seemed to be accepting the situation at last. He kept watching her, and she dared not even try to guess at the state of his mind.

"Tell me something, Kay. Was there any chance of you falling in love with me if you hadn't met Martin Searle?" His eyes glittered as he awaited her reply.

Kay sighed a little as she searched her mind, wanting to be truthful, and honest to herself.

"I don't think so," she said slowly. "I don't think so, Robin. If I had been going to fall in love with you it would have happened before this. I've known you six months at least. I was not feeling anything for you before I met Martin."

"Then you admit that you are interested in Searle." His tones roughened a little.

"I'm not admitting anything. Now you're twisting the questions around." She sighed again, and got to her feet. "We'd better get

180

on with your round," she said stiffly. "If you don't hurry it will be lunch-time before we're through."

He drained his cup and swallowed noisily, staring at her, his eyes bold and furious. She felt her mind shrivel a little as she watched him. He was pushing himself to his limits. His hands were trembling and he could hardly be recognised as the smart young doctor that he had been before last week-end. Even his clothes looked crumpled and uncared for.

They made the round together, and it was too easy for Kay to be aware of Robin's distress. She was on tenterhooks in case they should meet Matron around the corridors, for it seemed all too obvious to her that Robin was far from being himself, and she imagined that everyone else would be able to notice it too.

But their duty passed off without incident, although Robin was a bit short with some of the patients when they asked the usual questions about their progress. There was a snap in his voice that Kay had never heard before, and his manner was brusque and unsympathetic.

When they parted, Kay went along to her office, and she was appalled by the lateness of the hour. She would have to work very much harder in the next two or three hours in order to catch up. She sat at her desk to attend to the interminable paperwork, and there was no time for her to give Martin any thought.

After lunch she set to with a will, and as there were no emergencies or interruptions she managed to make some headway with her backlog of work. From time to time she had to get away from her desk to continue her own duty around the Clinic, and she went along to Mrs. Grover's room every half hour in order to check on the woman. More often than not Mrs. Grover was asleep, or pretending to be, and Kay did not disturb her. But she noticed some of the colour filling the patient's cheeks, and there were high hopes in Kay's heart as she went on with her work.

The afternoon became busy at tea-time, and all hands had to help with the patients' meal. It was always a mad rush after to the time of going off duty, and in the last half hour Kay found thoughts of Martin beginning to intrude upon her mind again. She was filled with pleasant anticipation, and finally went off duty with a great sigh of relief that the day, as far as the Clinic was concerned, was over.

After the seemingly long day, time began

to pass more quickly, or seemed to, and she had hardly managed to change out of her uniform and prepare to go out when she realised that Martin would be arriving at any moment. Her heart seemed to be singing as she went down to the hall to await the arrival of his car.

Robin came along the ground floor corridor while she stood there, and although he pretended to be surprised at sight of her, she had the feeling that he'd come by at that precise moment because he knew she would be there. But he seemed quite pleasant, and actually smiled at her as she opened the door and walked out of the Clinic in order to get away from him. She stood outside in the wan sunlight that was rapidly fading, looking at the crowds of tulips and daffodils that were already blooming in the flower beds. It would soon be Easter, she told herself in some surprise, and felt uplifted that summer would not be far behind. She walked across the terrace to the side of the main door and descended the steps to look more closely at the flowers. There were blue and yellow crocuses in great clusters around small rockeries in the main beds, and they gave a brave show of colour in the hostile wind.

The sound of a car attracted her attention and she looked up to see Martin's car coming along the driveway. For some unknown reason she turned and studied the tiers of windows in the front of the Clinic, suspecting that Robin would be at one of them to watch her leave. But she saw nothing because the last of the sunlight was playing on the windows, and she pursed her lips and walked along the gravelled path to where Martin had stopped the car.

"Hello, Kay!" He sounded very pleased to see her, and his smiling face was a tonic that instantly halted her brooding thoughts and worrying concern.

"Martin, it's been such a long day." She almost scrambled into the car in her eagerness. She smiled and promptly forgot about the day, and Martin slid an arm around her shoulders very briefly.

"What would you like to do this evening?" he asked tenderly.

"This evening!" She sat silent for a moment, thinking. She hadn't let her mind get so far ahead during the day. But she smiled at him, and saw his face take on an expression of tenderness. "I don't mind, so long as I'm with you. Take me where you will."

"I'd like to take you a long way from here," he said, looking into her eyes. "You're really beautiful, Kay. Hasn't anyone ever told you that?"

She smiled, and he leaned sideways to kiss her.

"Oh, not here, Martin!"

"Why not? It doesn't matter, surely. You're off duty!"

She recalled Matron's words of that morning in connection with the incident that had occurred the previous night, and a sigh gusted through her.

"I'm off duty, but there may be nurses looking from the windows, Martin."

"So?" He sounded truculent for some reason. "It's none of their business what you do when off duty, surely. You're stifled as it is with petty regulations, aren't you?"

"It's not so bad here at the Clinic," she said gently.

He smiled thinly and started the car, driving away swiftly, and Kay settled back and tried to relax. But despite Martin's smile and cheerful greeting, Kay sensed that all was not right with his world, and a frown touched her smooth forehead and her eyes dulled a little.

"How's your grandmother?" she enquired.

"Fine, thanks. She was asking after you, and sends her regards. When I told her we'd be going out for the afternoon tomorrow she wanted to know if she could go with us."

"Why not? Is there any reason why she shouldn't?"

"None at all! It would do her good. I can't remember the last time she went for a drive with me." He glanced swiftly at her. "We could go for a drive, couldn't we?"

"Anything you wish. I'm very easy to please." She looked into his eyes as he glanced at her, and she saw uneasiness there. "What's wrong?" she demanded instantly.

"Wrong?" He smiled thinly. "Why should you think there is anything wrong?"

"I can sense it." She began to feel a pang of worry inside. "Out with it, Martin. Don't keep it to yourself."

He drove fast along the road, keeping his eyes ahead. She studied his face, telling herself automatically how much she loved him. Darkness was clawing into the sky, but far away, still struggling desperately to overcome the long domination of the day. Fleecy clouds were sailing on high, like ghostly schooners on spirited voyages across the trackless heavens, and long golden fingers were raking them like searchlights as the sun declared itself vanquished and seemed to tip below the distant horizon. It was a tense but beautiful moment for Kay, and she felt many strange emotions flit inside her.

186

But she knew there was something wrong with Martin, and she was determined to find out what it was . . .

ELEVEN

Martin said nothing to alarm Kay during the evening, although she was certain he had something on his mind. But they made plans for the next afternoon, and when they returned later to the Clinic he stopped the car and they sat in the darkness for some time, just chatting quietly. Kay wanted to ask direct questions, but felt afraid to for fear that she might learn something she did not wish to know. Her instincts were warning her that Martin had something on his mind which concerned her, and it hadn't been there the evening before.

"Well it's time for you to go in again, Kay," he said at length, stifling a sigh as he prepared to drive her the rest of the way to the Clinic. "These evenings pass all too quickly, don't they?"

She agreed, and was aware that he hadn't taken her into his arms firmly and kissed her passionately. He had held her close, but his arms seemed to lack the warmth of previous embraces, and his lips had lacked fire. She was despondent as he entered the driveway and drove halfway along its length before stopping again.

"Shall I come up to the house to pick you up tomorrow, Kay?" he demanded.

"Yes." She nodded, relieved that at least he would be coming for her. But she realised with some hope that perhaps he was worried about something else. She naturally thought she was the cause for his disquiet, but that might not be the case. His grandmother might be on his mind, or perhaps there were business worries.

"Goodnight!" His lips brushed her cheek. "I'll arrive at two-thirty for you tomorrow, Kay."

"Goodnight," she replied, and got hastily from the car, feeling a little hurt by his coolness and angry with herself for not finding the courage to tax him about his mood. She stepped back while he turned the car around, and waved when he glanced at her before driving off, and when he had gone from sight she let her shoulders slump and her mind filled with concern.

As she walked along under the trees, intent upon gaining the Clinic as quickly as possible, she looked around for the first sign of Robin

Kent, recalling his behaviour of the previous night. She sighed heavily as she considered the long day that lay behind her. It was a day that would live in her mind for a very long time, and she didn't think she would be able to face another like it.

She reached the house without incident, and gave a long sigh of relief as she entered. Perhaps Robin had learned his lesson. At least she didn't have to wonder whether he would leap out of the bushes at her every time she came in after dark.

When she reached the sanctuary of her room, Kay sank down upon her bed and heaved a long, long, sigh. She felt very near to tears, as if her subconscious mind was aware of the reason for Martin's coldness and had already reached a decision about her future, but she had no real idea what lay beyond his mood. He had been worried by something, that much had been clear, but the reasons for it were not in her hands.

She fell asleep wondering about Martin, and awakened next morning with him still very much in her thoughts. Dressing, she went along to breakfast, and sat thoughtful and rather serious-minded while she ate. Then she went on duty, and felt as if she had stepped out of a prison as she applied herself to her work. Her mind cleared and she felt

189

happier. Martin slipped into the background of her thoughts and she was content to let him rest there. But she could not forget that she was seeing him that afternoon, and there was a strange relief inside her when she recalled that Mrs. Cameron-Boyd was going with them.

Making her first round of the day, Kay found Gordon Taylor awake and rather alert in his bed. He looked up at her with dark eyes that seemed to burn in his pale face, and Kay realised it was the first time she had seen him fully conscious since he had been admitted on Sunday.

"Good morning, Mr. Taylor," she greeted cheerfully, going to the foot of the bed. "It's nice to see you taking notice. How are you feeling now?"

"Better than I've been for a very long time, Sister," he replied in quiet tones. "The doctor hasn't said anything to me yet, but I've got the feeling that I'm on the mend. You were present at the operation, so Nurse Upton tells me. What happened?"

"I'm sure the doctor wouldn't want me to tell you anything. He will explain everything you need to know when he feels that you are fit to listen. All you have to do right now is lie there and rest and get well, and we're going to do all we can to help you. I will tell you this much. You're on the road to recovery now. It's entirely up to you how much progress you make. Rest and quiet is what you need, so don't worry yourself with questions."

"I shan't worry any more," he said quietly. "I was worried sick for months before the operation. My relief now is terrific. I feel different. The headaches have gone. I feel like a man who's been given a new lease of life."

Kay let pictures of the operation slip back into her mind, and she knew he must be feeling wonderful. He certainly had been given a new lease of life! That tumour would certainly have killed him had it not been removed.

"I'm fifty years old," Gordon Taylor went on. "I'd given up all hope. I wasn't so concerned for myself, but if I'd died there would have been my wife and daughter. I'm glad for their sake, Sister."

"And I'm glad for your sake, Mr. Taylor," Kay told him as she departed.

She thought of the man for some time while she made her round. It gave her a great feeling of satisfaction to know that she had been part of the team that had undoubtedly saved his life. She looked down at her hands as she neared Mrs. Grover's room, and she took her mind off Gordon Taylor and began to wonder what else she could do for Mrs. Grover. Entering the woman's room, Kay found her sitting up in bed, staring at the distant scene on the other side of the tall window, and for a moment there was silence while they looked at one another.

Kay studied Mrs. Grover's face, trying to read something in the other's pale expression. She could only hope that her words of yesterday had been of some help.

"How are you this morning, Mrs. Grover?" she enquired.

"I'm feeling well in myself, Sister," came the steady reply.

"Good. Have you got over the effects of the aspirin?"

There was silence for a moment, and a shadow seemed to cross the woman's face. No doubt the thought of the incident was painful, but Kay felt it right to talk naturally about what had happened.

"Yes, thank you. I'm feeling a lot better." There was a slight pause. "I think the talking-to that you gave me yesterday was a real tonic, Sister. I must confess that I haven't liked you while I've been here. You've always been sharp towards me, and I thought you were without sympathy. But after yesterday I can see that you've always been a great help. You've known exactly what manner to use in handling me, and I want to thank you for the way you spoke to me yesterday. I think you've done the trick. I was very thoughtful all yesterday, and for the first time since my husband's death I've been able to look outwards, away from myself. You showed me the way! I think I'm going to be all right."

"I hope so, Mrs. Grover!" Kay smiled slowly. She didn't take her eyes from the woman's face. "You'll find there will be difficult days ahead for you. It won't come right just like that. You'll have to work hard at standing on your own feet again. But remember that while you're here we will do what we can to help you."

"I shan't ever forget that," Mrs. Grover said eagerly. "I admire you, Sister."

Kay smiled as she went on her way. Moments like that made all the difference in a nurse's life. She was feeling pretty pleased with herself as she went back to her office. Duty was hard at times, and wearing on the nerves, but the results made everything worthwhile.

She had just sat down at her desk when Miss Stokes appeared in the doorway, where she paused for a moment before entering the office. Kay looked up at her superior, and a little trace of colour came to her cheeks. She knew she would never be able to forget being caught by Matron in Robin Kent's embrace, and she had the feeling that Miss Stokes wouldn't forget it either.

"I'd like to have a word with you, Sister," Matron said rather sternly, and Kay tensed as she nodded. Miss Stokes closed the door of the office and came to confront Kay across the desk. "I know this is none of my business, Sister," she went on slowly, holding Kay's eyes with the power of her own. "What a nurse does off duty is no concern of mine. I have no wish to hark back to the night before last when I was checking the grounds. That, too, is no business of mine. But the conduct of Doctor Kent while he is on duty does concern me, and I am rather perturbed at his recent behaviour around the Clinic. No doubt you have noticed that he's been drinking, and although I am not prepared to tackle him on that subject, I'm equally sure that Professor Alden would have a great deal to say about it."

"Doctor Kent's behaviour is not my responsibility, Matron," Kay said softly.

"I know." Miss Stokes nodded worriedly. "But I can't help feeling that you are responsible for the way he's behaving. I've noticed that he seems to be in love with you. I don't wish to pry into your affairs, Sister, but am I right in thinking that you have turned him down and that's what is upsetting him?"

"That's it exactly, Matron!" Kay could see no reason for not telling the truth. "I've been rather worried about him myself, but there's nothing I can do to help him."

"I understand. I have heard rumours about you, Sister. About you and Martin Searle, that is!" Matron smiled. "I wish you all the luck in the world."

"What can we do about Doctor Kent, Matron?"

"I don't know." Miss Stokes shook her head slowly, and her face was set in uneasy lines. "He's been such a good doctor that it will be a pity if this business throws him completely."

"It isn't my fault, Matron," Kay said in rather worried tones. "I didn't know he felt that way about me until after I had met Mr. Searle. But even if I hadn't met him, Doctor Kent wouldn't have been the man I'd choose."

"A girl has the right to choose the man she wants, Sister. I am not blaming you for Doctor Kent's predicament. I'm just wondering if it might not be better if you had a word with him rather than me. Anything coming from me does tend to sound official, and I wouldn't want him jumping to conclusions. That might make him even worse."

"What would you want me to say to him?"

"Just tell him he's beginning to make a fool of himself."

"I've already done that. He said that he might consider looking for another position."

"So it is as bad as that!" Miss Stokes shook her head slowly as she looked into Kay's eyes.

"Would you rather I left, Matron?" she asked.

"You! Good Lord no! We could always get another doctor in here. But I doubt if we could ever replace you, Sister. Don't give that another thought, please."

"I do feel responsible, Matron."

"Perhaps you do. It would be natural, I suppose. But you mustn't blame yourself under any circumstances. If Doctor Kent wants to leave us then he is at liberty to do so, but he must also behave himself until he goes."

"I'll have another talk to him, Matron."

"Good. I was hoping you would. It will sound better coming from you."

"Would you want me to mention that you are aware of his behaviour?" Kay watched her superior's face with intent gaze.

"Perhaps not yet. Let's try and ease him

back on the right path without making too much of it. If we can't do it that way then I shall have to speak to him myself."

"I'm off duty this afternoon and all tomorrow, Matron."

"Of course! But don't worry about this. I expect you do feel responsible if only because Doctor Kent has fallen in love with you. But you're not to blame, and if you remember that you won't start giving yourself a neurosis."

Kay smiled thinly as Matron turned to depart. She summed up the whole situation in much the same way that Miss Stokes had. But it was easy for Matron to say don't worry. One wouldn't be human if one could dismiss the whole thing as if it had never happened.

When Matron had departed, Kay sat for a moment thinking about Martin, and there was a thread of worry in her mind that writhed like an angry snake. She could fully understand how Robin was feeling, for the same worries, although on a much smaller scale, were present in her mind when she took the time to think of Martin's cold mood the evening before. She looked at the clock and counted the hours to the moment when Martin would be calling for her, and she could feel her soul chafing at the impatience building up in her breast.

197

She forced herself to forget about the whole painful subject, but her feelings were too powerful for her, and they began to bubble furiously as if in complete disobedience to her wishes.

When Robin appeared to take his morning round, Kay had a bad moment. She looked into his face, hoping that a miracle had occurred in the night to remove all thoughts of her from his mind. But she saw the agony in his dark eyes and knew he was still losing the fight that he was obviously making against her. He stared at her eagerly, as if he had forgotten what she looked like, and a hungry expression filtered into his face. He took a deep breath and paused in the doorway.

"Good morning, Doctor," she said awkwardly, wondering just how to address him now. She was rather relieved when Nurse Upton appeared behind him, having obviously waited for his appearance.

"Doctor," the girl said rather quickly. "Mrs. Grover is asking for you."

Kay looked into Robin's face. He was so serious, and yet his face had been made for laughter. Recalling how happy he had always been before Martin came into her life, she felt a sharp pang of conscience. But she knew she ought not to blame herself.

"Go along and tell Mrs. Grover that I'll see her presently," he ordered, and Nurse Upton nodded and hurried away. "I want to talk to you first, Kay," he added.

She said nothing, but placed her hands carefully on the desk before her, looking down at them. She felt so guilty whenever she met his gaze.

"We have nothing to talk about," she said softly.

"We have nothing to talk about ourselves," he said in small, precise tones. His expression hardened. "I want to talk about the patients."

"I'm sorry! Of course." She felt put in her place, and she knew she couldn't broach the subject of Matron's conversation with him. He was becoming unapproachable, and this was another sign that the situation between them would get worse and worse.

"About Mrs. Grover," he said, not meeting her gaze. "I want a full report on even the slightest change in her mental condition."

"Well I'm happy to report that for once Mrs. Grover is seeming optimistic." Kay told him of her conversation with the woman earlier.

"That's a good sign," he said grudgingly. "Keep up the good work. I have the feeling that I can help her a great deal, and I have a good mind to take a personal interest in her just to pull her through the awkward moments." He spoke musingly, and Kay knew she ought not to have heard his words. His lips tightened as he looked at her, and then he nodded. "I'll go along and talk to Mrs. Grover alone," he said. "When I get through with her I'll come back for you, and we'll make the routine round."

"Yes, Doctor," she said slowly.

He stared coolly into her eyes for a moment, then turned and departed, and Kay felt numb inside, hurt in the way that a small child is hurt when her face is slapped for no good reason.

But anything would be better than his former manner, when he drank on duty and chased after her, his passions out of control and his mind afire with desire for her. If only he would become interested in Mrs. Grover, Kay thought speculatively. Everyone would benefit! But she dismissed the thought before it could take root. Personal relationships between staff and patients were frowned upon, and definitely discouraged. Robin might find himself in much more trouble if he began looking too hard at Mrs. Grover.

She remained in the office until Robin came for her some fifteen minutes later. He seemed a little easier, and actually smiled when he paused to look at her.

"I'm ready to make the round now, Sister," he said formally.

She got to her feet and moved obediently to the door, and he stepped outside and led the way, his shoulders held stiffly, and that was the only sign of emotion in him.

They didn't go into Mrs. Grover's room on their way round the patients, and Kay made a mental note to visit the woman as soon as Robin had departed. They completed the round thirty minutes late, and already in the kitchen they were thinking of lunch for the patients. When she got back to her office, Kay had to go through the diet sheets, and she tried to keep one eye on the clock as she hurried to regain some of her lost time. She couldn't get away to check on Mrs. Grover, and before she knew it, lunch was being served.

It was always a hectic time, getting the food around to the patients before it was cold, and Kay felt like a limp rag by the time everyone had been served. But she could not stop. Going off duty at one meant that she had to make up her reports, and she tried to do this exacting chore while attending to other things.

Now it seemed that the hands of the clock slipped round of their own volition. She was eager to get off duty in order to prepare to meet Martin, and yet she felt reluctant to see him for she felt that he had bad news to impart. He had given her that impression the night before. But he had not been able to bring himself to the point of speaking. However with another night of considering behind him he might now have decided what to do, and she intuitively felt that there would be bad news for her at some time during the remainder of the day.

Matron relieved her when it was time for her to depart, and Kay heaved a long sigh of relief as she went up to her quarters. There was a deep trembling inside her that tried to unseat the balance of her nerves. She found herself wondering what had happened to the great happiness she had experienced only a few days ago. What had happened to rob her of that great joy?

By the time she had eaten her lunch and changed to go out it was almost time for Martin to arrive, and she went to her window and looked down at the driveway, watching for the first sight of Martin's car. She pictured his face in her mind while she waited, and her heart was heavy as she imagined that the first bright rapture which had taken them was now waning and fading.

But the sight of Martin's car approaching

restored her high spirits, and her eyes glistened as she stared at it for a moment, just to make sure. When she was certain she took up her handbag and hurriedly left the room, almost running down the stairs in order to be at the door by the time the car stopped, and she was breathless as she went outside, to find Martin sitting behind the wheel, his window down and the sunlight bathing him. He smiled at her as she approached him, and she felt her heart bound like a fawn in the forest. If only there was nothing to worry about! The thought stabbed through her as she reached the car, and she looked critically into his face as she got in beside him.

"Hello," she said, and there was almost a trace of shyness in her tones.

"Hello, Kay. How are you today?" He didn't seem anything but normal, and his face was gentle, his blue eyes soft and filled with light.

"It's been a bit of a rush," she admitted, settling herself at his side.

"We're going to be on our own," he retorted. "Grandmother is feeling a bit unsteady today so we shan't risk it by taking her along. I think the anticipation really upset her, so we'll give her the chance to think about going out a little more before we actually take the plunge with her."

"Oh, I'm sorry! A trip out in the car would have made all the difference to her! What a pity! Shall we go back to Cameron Glen and keep her company?"

"No." He shook his head, starting the car quickly. "She was insistent upon us going on as planned. She wouldn't hear of us staying behind with her."

Kay stared ahead as they left the Clinic, and her mind was filled with conjecture. Was she going to learn anything to their mutual disadvantage? Had he found a change of heart where she was concerned? She suddenly knew that she had to find out. She could not go on wondering, spoiling her sleep with dark thoughts. Before the day was out, she told herself finally, she would ask him point blank what was troubling him, and she didn't think for one moment that she would like the answer.

But they could enjoy themselves before she gave him the opportunity to speak. If he was looking for a way to broach any unpleasant subject then she would give him one. Her sudden determination filled her with dejection, and tears stung her eyes for a moment, and she had to blink them rapidly away.

They left the Clinic and went on across

the wide, desolate moors, and the sense of loneliness that was innate with Kay seemed to rise up within to choke her. She suppressed a sigh as she leaned towards him, wanting to get as near to him as was possible without touching him. But he was intent upon his driving and she could sense the stiffness that was in him, the intangible coldness that was erecting barriers between them. It wasn't imagination, she told herself swiftly. She knew there was trouble between them as surely as if he had already told her.

TWELVE

The afternoon was perfect in the way that only early spring could make it. There was a sense of buoyancy in the air, of expectancy, as if Nature was awaiting the return of the sun before commencing seasonal activities, but already there were signs of movement in the buds on the trees and bushes, the growing crispness in the turf, the notes of optimism in the songs of the birds.

Kay felt her spirits rise as she looked about her. The moor seemed a haven of peace. Its desolate area was lonely, inviting to her and her present mental mood. But she could not find pure happiness, and she looked at Martin and wondered what was going on in his brain.

"Do you like this kind of an afternoon?" he asked. "Are you a girl who takes to the simple things of life or do you need the bright lights and a gay whirl of society?"

"This pleases me immensely," she said simply. "I wouldn't have to hesitate in making a choice between the bright lights and this sort of thing."

"I should have known from the way you came here in the first place just what kind of a girl you are." He didn't take his eyes from the road, and Kay looked at him, studying his face, trying to find some hint of what lay in his mind.

"What kind of a girl am I?" she demanded lightly.

"The kind of girl any man would be proud to know, would be fortunate to have as a friend."

"As a friend!" she echoed, and he glanced at her.

Silence followed for some moments, and Kay felt her hopes sinking. She took a deep breath and fought against indecision. She knew something was wrong and yet she was afraid to talk about it. But her uneasiness was growing all the time and she knew she would not be able to contain it.

"Martin, I have the feeling that something is troubling you!" The words forced themselves out of her mouth almost against her will, and as soon as she'd uttered them she was wishing she hadn't. But she was watching his face, and she saw his lips tighten.

"Troubling me?" he repeated, still staring ahead. "Why should you think that?"

"There's something different about you. I can't put my finger on it, but I noticed last night that you were rather quiet."

"I'm worried about Grandmother, if that's any help. She isn't so well, and I don't mean physically. She forgets things and imagines things."

"That is usual in very old people, Martin."

"I know. I don't suppose she has a great many years left to her. That much is obvious. But she's been going on and on for as long as I can remember."

"I thought there was something wrong which might have to do with me." She spoke slowly, carefully, and waited for his reply with bated breath.

He glanced at her, and his rather stern expression softened a little, but his eyes remained cool, calculating, and Kay frowned as she took in the signs of his uneasiness.

"What could possibly be troubling me that

has to do with you?" he demanded.

"I don't know!" It was easier to talk now the ice had been broken. "Is anything wrong, Martin?"

"No!" He shook his head. "I don't know what you're talking about, Kay."

But the very tone of his voice warned her that he was not telling the truth. A sigh quivered through her and she looked ahead for a moment, wondering how to get through to him.

"I have been thinking rather deeply about us, Kay," he began.

She looked at him quickly, knowing by his voice that he was about to give some hint of what was troubling him. But he didn't say anything, and his face was set, his eyes narrowed as he stared ahead. His hands were clenched tightly about the steering wheel, his knuckles showing white.

"Well?" she prompted gently.

"I have the feeling that I'm guilty of rushing you. We have not known each other a week yet!"

"Well?" Her chin came up. "What has time to do with it? I feel as if I've known you all my life. We're certainly not strangers to one another, are we? I mean, we don't feel like strangers."

"I'll grant you that!" He nodded slowly.

"But I'm going to put my foot on the brake where we are concerned, Kay. It would be a tragedy if things went wrong just because we were in too much of a hurry."

"I'm not in any hurry at all." She was cold inside, as if a chill wind was blowing through her heart.

He glanced at her, and she saw him moisten his lips. She clenched her hands in her lap and set her teeth into her bottom lip, relishing the pain she derived from the action.

"I hope you understand me!" He sounded awkward. "I don't know how to put it, but we would be extremely foolish if we rushed headlong into anything."

"Martin, I don't know what you mean! How can we rush into anything? We're very good friends. We came together naturally, and we seem to be ideally suited. That's what makes us take to each other so well. But there's never been any suggestion that we grow impatient and rush things. I'm not looking into the future. I'm getting too much out of the present to want to do that. I'm quite content to see you and let things take their natural course, if you are! But if you think you've made a complete mistake and that we shouldn't see each other again then say so, or turn the car around and take me back to the Clinic!"

"I knew you wouldn't understand!" He sighed sharply. "You have taken the wrong interpretation, Kay. I certainly haven't made a mistake about you. There could never be any other girl for me, not after meeting you! I'm in love with you! It came naturally, and quickly. I have the feeling that we were meant for each other."

"Then why this attitude?" She twisted in her seat to face him. "Martin, what's wrong? If you haven't any doubts about us then what has induced this attitude in you?"

He glanced at her, smiling wryly. "It seems that I met you too late, Kay. Perhaps I shouldn't tell you this, but I know you have become infatuated by me. I can see it in your eyes. I've made you forget your duty and your past. But although I want you so badly, although I know you're right for me, I can't take you on these conditions. We've got to wait until you find your true feelings. In a week or so this infatuation may wear off, and then we'd both be sorry for what is happening."

"I just don't understand what you're getting at!" She frowned as she watched his face. "You're not making sense, Martin. Look, if you think you've made a mistake then say so, and I'll go back to the Clinic and we'll forget all about this."

She caught her breath as a lump came into her throat, but she hardened herself against her emotions.

"I hardly like to drag it out into the open," he said reluctantly. "But Dr. Kent telephoned me yesterday. He told me that the two of you are almost engaged, and he said you'd told him that you couldn't help yourself where I'm concerned. He asked me to let you go, that the two of you were in love and had been so for a number of months. He said your career was in jeopardy now, and so was his. He seemed to think that if I was in love with you then I ought to be ready to make the sacrifice for you. If I let you alone then everything would be all right again."

Kay stared at him, the sound of his bleak tones slashing through her mind. She caught her breath as the full import of what he said got through to her. But she was speechless with amazement, and her mind seemed to freeze as she tried to answer him. Finally, a laugh tore itself free from her throat, and Martin looked at her in growing surprise.

"It's no laughing matter!" he said sharply. "If you were in love with Kent then you shouldn't have let yourself come under my spell."

"I certainly did that, didn't I?" She shook

211

her head. "So that's as low as Robin Kent can sink, is it?"

"What do you mean?"

"I've never been in love with Robin Kent in my life!" She began to tell him of the true situation that existed between Robin and herself, and she watched his face, hoping to see relief and pleasure, but afraid that he wouldn't accept her words. When she fell silent he drew a sharp breath. "Well?" she demanded anxiously. "You do believe me, don't you?"

"I want to believe you more than anything in the world," he retorted. "But I can't risk breaking your career. I know how much it means to you, Kay."

"Nothing means anything to me except you," she said boldly.

"This is exactly what Dr. Kent was saying. You've become blinded by your emotions. You won't accept any rational explanation."

"There's only one thing to do," she said firmly. "Turn the car around and take me back to the Clinic!"

He slowed the car, then stopped on the side of the road. He turned to her, looking intently into her face.

"Kay, I wouldn't want to do anything but what is right for you, no matter how it hurt me. I'd take you back to the Clinic now and never see you again if I thought it was the right thing to do."

"Martin, can't you understand? Robin Kent is in love with me. I've known for some time. But I'm not in love with him. He is the one who's started going to pieces. He's beginning to come on duty much the worse for wear; drinking heavily and losing his temper. He lied to you. He knows I'm in love with you and he wants to do anything he can to part us, even though he knows I'm not in love with him. Surely you're not going to believe anything he says! He's a jealous man, and not to be trusted."

He shook his head slowly and sighed heavily. "I wouldn't want to be a dog in a manger, Kay."

"Take me back to the Clinic, Martin," she commanded firmly. "I'll get Robin out to talk to you. He won't lie while I'm confronting him!"

"I'm not going to take part in any emotional scene," he said hastily.

She watched him for a moment, dread stealing into her heart. His face showed something of his mental attitude, and she knew Robin Kent had poisoned his mind.

"All right," she said slowly. "Take me back to the Clinic and leave it at that."

"Do you mean that?"

213

"Of course! In my job I daren't let my personal life intrude upon duty. If you're not going to see reason in this then we'd better call it a day."

He shook his head. "Are you telling me that Dr. Kent would ring me and deliberately lie about you?"

"That's what he's done." She sat straight in her seat and stared ahead, her face set and her mind closed to contain the misery that was beginning to overpower her. "I've never had the slightest feeling for him. He's so jealous now that he would say and do anything to put an end to us." She glanced at him, her tones softening. "You don't have to take my word for it, Martin. Ask anyone at the Clinic. They'll all tell you that there's been nothing between Robin Kent and me."

"I couldn't do that, could I?" He shook his head slowly. "I thought everything was going too well for us. We haven't known each other a week yet and we made too much progress in the first day or so."

"I disagree with you. We met and found a certain level. Perhaps other people wouldn't have reached the same level for months, but we didn't rush anything. It was all so natural."

"I ought to have a word with Dr. Kent," Martin began.

214

Kay turned to him, reaching out and taking hold of his hand. He shook his head slowly and sighed heavily, and then turned to her and swept her into his arms. He kissed her passionately, and Kay felt relief stealing back into her. She clung to him, throwing off the cloud of black depression which had hung over her. She knew by his lips and his kisses that he wasn't falling out of love with her or having second thoughts. Robin Kent had driven a small wedge between them.

"Martin, can't you tell that Dr. Kent was lying to you?"

"I want to believe that more than anything else in the world," he retorted. "I'd do anything for you, Kay, including never seeing you again, if it would help."

"It would break my heart," she retorted. "Don't ever consider that."

He nodded, smiling now, although his eyes were still troubled. She pressed her face against his shoulder, closing her eyes and praying that all would be well. She would be unhappy for the rest of her life if anything happened to part them. She clenched her teeth when she thought of Robin Kent, and she determined to give him a piece of her mind when she saw him again.

"Kay, I love you," Martin said softly.

"Oh, Martin! I don't know what I'd do if

215

you stayed away from me."

"Look, let's forget about it this afternoon. You've got the time off and you ought to be able to relax and enjoy yourself. I don't care what Kent had to say. You're with me now and I'm going to give you a good time."

She nodded, and he kissed her again, hugging her with all his strength. Kay felt tears start into her eyes, and she blinked rapidly. She hadn't imagined that Robin Kent could be so mean, but his actions had really pinpointed the deep feelings he held for her.

They went on, and Kay felt much happier. Martin took her to a ruined abbey, and they spent a pleasant hour wandering around the ruins and wondering about the past. This sort of excursion was a great source of pleasure to Kay. She relished the peaceful surroundings, the remains of a people long dead, the air of remoteness that always came to her when in the presence of history, and when Martin drew her into a lonely corner and took her into his arms she felt her relief and joy swell to bursting point.

"You look happier now than when I first collected you," he said, holding her close.

"That's because I knew something was bothering you, and it made me think I might lose you," she replied. "But forget about that, Martin. There was no truth at all in what

Robin Kent told you."

"I had no course but to believe him! If he hadn't been telling the truth then there was no point in contacting me at all, was there? That's the way I looked at it. If he split us up you wouldn't have gone back to him if you hadn't been with him before you met me. I hope I'm making myself clear, Kay!" He looked down anxiously into her face.

"Why not forget all about it, Martin?" she suggested, and saw him nod slowly.

"We'll do that," he promised. "Come on, let's get back into the car. It's going to rain."

"No." She pulled at him as he started to lead her away. "Let's stay here! It's sheltered."

He narrowed his eyes as he stared at her upturned face, and then he nodded slowly. Kay moistened her lips and he kissed her. The atmosphere had turned gloomy, and there was a black cloud pushing forward to hide the sun. A chill breeze leaped up from nowhere and sent a shiver through Kay as it attacked her spitefully. But Martin put his arms around her and held her close. Together they watched an advancing line of rain coming across the moors like a wall of mist, and soon the first large drops arrived, beating down solidly upon the thick ruined walls.

"This is crazy," Martin said softly, pressing

his face against the top of her head.

"We're not getting wet." Kay peeped around him at the driving rain, and saw that they were completely cut off from reality. The high stone walls, crumbling under the ceaseless attacks of time itself, were indistinct about them, protecting them against the elements in much the same way that they must have protected many people through the ages, from many dangers. "I like the feeling it gives me, being trapped here away from the rest of the world."

He nodded his understanding and pulled her even closer into his arms.

"I love you, Kay," he said softly, taking her chin in his hand and gently tilting her face so he could look into her eyes. "I can't fault you anywhere. No matter how I test you I can't find a single reason for doubting that you are made for me."

"You can tell me that sort of thing all day and I wouldn't get tired of listening," she answered softly. "Go on, tell me more."

He did, holding her close and whispering gently, in the way that lovers had done through the centuries, and Kay could not help wondering just how many times these old ruins had witnessed similar incidents. Time seemed to fade away, and there were no reminders that responsibilities and obligations awaited them upon their return to civilisation.

How long they remained under cover from the driving rain, soothed by its gentle insistence upon the ground, Kay did not know. Now and again a bolder drop of water would splatter against her face or Martin's head, but they were not getting wet, and the chillness that seeped into the atmosphere did not touch them as they stood so close together. Kay wished they could have gone on standing here for the rest of time, but eventually the rain eased and Martin glanced at his watch.

"It's almost five-thirty," he declared. "Aren't you hungry?"

"Just a little," she admitted.

"Then let's go across the moors to a little village I know. When you enter the village you'll think you've gone back in time to the fifteenth century. We'll have tea there in an olde worlde café, and afterwards – well, afterwards, you can decide what we'll do."

"That sounds simply wonderful," she whispered, taking his arm as they started towards the car, their feet splashing through the wet grass. "I'm thoroughly enjoying this!"

"And tomorrow isn't touched yet!" he retorted in pleased tones. "You have the whole day off and we can go where we please." His arm tightened about her shoulders as they approached the car. "I love you, Kay. No matter what happens, always remember that I love you."

"You can tell me every day," she whispered, and he held her close before opening the door of the car for her. In that moment she knew supreme happiness, and she found herself hoping desperately that nothing would ever rob her of this memory, that nothing would ever come between them and their strangely powerful love . . .

THIRTEEN

Kay was completely restored to happiness by the time Martin returned her to the Clinic that evening, and the next day, Friday, they spent together, firmly cementing what had appeared to be a breach in their association. By the time Friday came to an end and they returned to the Clinic, Kay was beside herself with joy. She had been certain of her love for Martin before the day began, but now an extra depth seemed to have been added, and her mind was like a bottomless pit, filled with all the good impressions and happy emotions.

When Martin brought the car to a halt in the driveway of the Clinic, Kay sighed heavily and began to bring her mind back from ecstasy. She felt reluctant to leave him, and when she looked into his face she saw the same reluctance there.

"I don't want to let you go," he whispered, stroking her hair. "I love you, Kay. A lot has happened to me since yesterday afternoon. I know now that no other girl could ever step into your place in my heart. I agree with you that time does not matter. It still isn't a week since we first met, but you've been in my mind from the day I was born. I've been subconsciously looking for you ever since I was old enough to dream about you. Don't let anything ever come between us, my dearest."

"Martin!" His name was like a prayer on her lips. "I love you. Now that we have cleared the air between us nothing can ever touch us." She glanced towards the Clinic, where only a few lights shone from some of the many windows. There were dark shadows all about them, screening them, acting as a benevolent cloak to shield them against the rest of the world. They had been remote all day, and Kay was filled with the kind of reverence that comes during a visit to a cathedral. "Robin Kent can't do any more harm between us, can he?"

"He won't." Martin spoke firmly. "I've a good mind to give him a call and tell him what I think of him, but I suppose it would be better to forget all about it. One can't blame him for trying everything to win you. I would probably have done the same thing if I had been in his shoes. It's a compliment to you, really, Kay, the way he's been trying to get you, and I do feel sorry for him. I know how I would feel if I ever lost you."

She went into his arms for a goodnight kiss, and closed her eyes as she relaxed in his embrace. His mouth held a great deal of promise, and she could hardly control her imagination. Now she was beginning to look into the future, and her hopes were set high, confidently high.

"I really must go in now, Martin," she said at length. "I'm on duty tomorrow."

"When shall I see you again?"

"Whenever you want."

"I know, dearest, but when will you be free?"

"Tomorrow evening? I'll be free at about seven."

"I'll call for you! We've got to celebrate tomorrow evening, you know."

"Celebrate?" she demanded, frowning.

"It's our first anniversary! It's a week tomorrow that we met!" He was smiling as he spoke, and she could see the love in his eyes.

"We're going to do a lot of celebrating in

our lives, by all indications," she retorted, laughing, and he held her close once more.

"I sincerely hope so," he said. "Life is going to be one long celebration now I've met you."

They parted then, reluctantly and slowly, and Kay watched him drive away, her mind filled with wonderful thoughts. When he had gone she turned and walked up to the Clinic, going into the building quietly and making her way to her room. She was still out of touch with reality when she went to bed, and it wasn't until next morning when she arose that she found her feet firmly upon the ground.

Routine in the morning set her mind straight and she had to push all her personal thoughts out of her mind. It was difficult to stop thinking of Martin, but she attacked her work with great effort, and had the nurses running around as well as they went through their morning routines.

When she dropped into Mrs. Grover's room she was surprised to see the woman up and dressed, seated by the window and staring out at the scenery.

"Well, this is a surprise," Kay said pleasantly, and Mrs. Grover looked at her and smiled. "That talk we had the other morning has worked wonders if this is the result of it."

"You certainly helped, Sister, but it's Doctor Kent who's applying the therapy now. I'm thinking of opening a Clinic similar to this one, probably in Wales, and Doctor Kent will run it for me."

"Really!" Kay frowned as she let the import of what had been said sink into her mind. "I know that Doctor Kent is thinking of leaving here. You wouldn't find a more suitable man for the position he would fill in your Clinic."

"I know. I'm sure it will be a good partnership. If it does nothing else, it's pulling me round, isn't it? I've not felt as optimistic as this for a long time. I'm sure I'm well enough to leave here now, and I can't wait to start making plans. I shall go to Wales and look for a suitable house, something about this size."

Kay smiled as she listened. She knew instinctively that they need not concern themselves any more about Mrs. Grover. She was not thinking of herself any more but concentrating upon other things, and this was all that was needed to make her well, to lift her up that last fraction to normalcy.

"I'll be happy to advise you in any way I can," Kay said as she turned to leave. "I can see that you don't need any pep talk from me now. I'm very happy for you, Mrs. Grover, and I hope you will find what you need. I wish you every success in your new venture."

"Thank you, Sister, and if you would consider leaving here I think we could give you the position of Matron in our Clinic."

"Thank you very much, but my whole future is tied up in this area." Kay smiled. "I'm sure you'll find someone suitable."

She was thoughtful as she left the woman's room and went back to her office. This seemed the ideal way out for all of them, Robin included. It would take him out of Scotland and out of Kay's life, and no doubt he would soon forget her, either under pressure of work at his new Clinic or because he would find someone else to take her place. It all seemed to be working out now, she thought as she sat down at her desk. She mentally crossed her fingers, and for a moment she fancied she could look into the future and see something of what her life would be like. She tingled inside with pleasure. Her wildest dreams seemed to be coming true. She sat with her mind lost in conjecture, and it wasn't until Miss Stokes spoke to her that she realised Matron was in the office with her.

"You were miles away, Sister," Miss Stokes said, smiling. "I hope I haven't dragged you back from some seventh heaven to a grim prison."

"It was nothing like that, Matron," Kay

replied with a smile.

"We can all do with dreaming a little from time to time," Miss Stokes said.

"But not while we're on duty, Matron," Kay added.

Matron sat down on the seat beside the desk. She studied Kay's face for a moment, noting the brightness of her eyes, the animation in every line of her face.

"I expect there will be some drastic changes around here before very long," she said. "I've just seen Mrs. Grover and she has informed me of her intention. While I agree this is the best possible medicine for the woman, I don't like the idea of Dr. Kent getting mixed up in it."

"You don't think he's qualified to run a place such as this?" Kay demanded.

"He has the necessary medical qualifications!" Miss Stokes emphasised, "but the human element in his case is not very promising. It is none of our business, of course, and under the circumstances it will be a relief to see him go, knowing his feelings for you, Sister. But I can't help feeling that he might be doing the wrong thing, especially with a woman like Mrs. Grover backing him."

"I hope it will work out for them," Kay said.

"I do, too. They have my sincerest wishes.

But you wouldn't go as Matron for them, would you?"

"I don't want to leave here, although that post was offered to me," Kay said with a smile.

"If you are keen to become a Matron then it's only fair to tell you that in a year or two I shall be leaving here, and you will be considered for the position."

"Really?" Kay caught her breath. It had always been the height of her ambitions to be called Matron in a place such as Braeside. But then she thought of Martin, and imagined that in another two years she might have left nursing for a more intimate career. She caught her breath at the thought, and her mind seemed to whirl under the pressures of her speculations.

"But all of that is still very much in the future, and your personal situation might change drastically in the time ahead. I think I can see some sort of indication in your face, Sister."

"My future seems to be very uncertain at the moment, Matron. This time last week I had my life all planned out, but that's all changed completely now."

"My congratulations, anyway, even if they are a trifle premature!"

"Thank you!" Kay smiled as Miss Stokes

arose and departed.

She sat for some time just thinking over what had been said. It was surprising how one's life could go on along the same old lines for year after year, then suddenly change completely and throw one into a series of complex situations that led into a whole new field of activity. She knew she was on the threshold of complete change, and she welcomed it.

When Robin appeared to make his round, Kay studied his face intently, and was pleasantly surprised to see that he had apparently recovered from his emotional troubles. He smiled lightly and dropped carelessly into the seat beside the desk.

"What about some coffee then?" he demanded.

"Have you time for it?"

"Certainly. I'm on top of the world this morning."

"Are congratulations in order?" Kay smiled at his swift change of expression. "Mrs. Grover told me first thing about her plans, and where you figure in them."

"She did?" He pulled a wry face. "I told her not to say anything at all about them."

"It's only natural that she should want to talk about it. It's doing her the world of good, Robin. And I hope it works out for your sake.

I'm glad you've got over me so quickly."

His face darkened for a moment and she saw the old sullen expression fleet across his features. But it was quickly gone and he smiled.

"It's all a matter of psychology, you know. I can keep you out of my mind so long as I have other interests."

"Mrs. Grover is a young woman," Kay ventured. "She can't be more than two or three years older than you. Perhaps something will happen to attract you to her."

"Not a chance," he scoffed. "When I look at you and think of what I'm missing! I'm only using her as a means to an end. I was thinking of leaving here to get away from you. She will be the means. I've always had ambitions to be the top man in a Clinic, and she's got a lot of money that she doesn't know what to do with. Well I'll help her put it to a good use."

Kay frowned at his bitter words. He seemed like a stranger again, and she didn't like the thoughts that began pushing into her mind. She heard a noise in the corridor and looked towards the door, expecting to see one of her nurses, but Mrs. Grover walked past, and didn't look into the office. Kay started to her feet, a frown touching her face. Had the woman overheard what Robin said? She went to the door, but when she looked out into the corridor she found that Mrs. Grover had disappeared from sight.

"Who was that?" Kent demanded.

"Mrs. Grover!"

"Oh Lord! Do you think she overheard me?"

"I don't know."

"Perhaps I'd better go back and have another word with her!"

"I wouldn't if I were you. It could only make matters worse. Forget about it, and guard your tongue in future." Kay was feeling angry with him and she let it show. But he merely shrugged and got to his feet.

"Come on," he said. "Let's do the round and get it over with."

Kay went with him, thoughtful and grave, and she was relieved when they had finished their duty together. Kent went off, and she walked back to Mrs. Grover's room, intent upon finding out if the woman had overheard anything that Robin Kent had said. But when she opened the door of the room she was surprised to find it empty. However Mrs. Grover was not confined to her room. She was now well enough to get around the Clinic as she wanted.

Going back to her office, Kay threw herself into her work in order to catch up with her schedule, and she forgot all about Mrs. Grover until it was time for the patients' lunch to be served. It was only when one of the nurses came to report that Mrs. Grover was nowhere to be seen that the woman returned to Kay's mind.

"She must be somewhere about the place," Kay said instantly. "Is she out in the grounds?"

"We've searched everywhere, Sister." Nurse Strawhorn was most certain.

Kay remembered her suspicions that Mrs. Grover might have overheard Robin Kent's bitter words concerning his intentions, and a pang struck through her as she considered.

"I'll have a word with Matron," she said. "Go about your duties, Nurse, and have another look around for Mrs. Grover if you can spare the time. Have you checked all the rooms? Is she with another patient?"

"She's not anywhere in the building," the nurse replied.

Kay telephoned Miss Stokes and explained the situation, and she mentioned the fact that the conversation in the office might have been overheard by their missing patient.

"Do you mean to tell me you think she might have overheard and taken it to heart? That she might have left the Clinic?"

"Well it certainly seems as if she isn't on

the premises," Kay said firmly.

"Can you describe what she was wearing?"

"She had on a dark two-piece costume when I saw her in the corridor," Kay said thoughtfully. "That's about all I noticed. She was going towards her room at that time. What she did after that I have no idea."

"Very well, Sister. Just check the place again, will you? Look everywhere, and report to me if you don't find her. But it is conceivable that she's slipped into town."

"How would she get into town?"

"She might have tried to get a lift on the road, or perhaps she set out to walk." Miss Stokes didn't sound too hopeful, and Kay replaced the receiver and hurried from the office.

She made a round of the Clinic herself, asking each patient if Mrs. Grover had been seen, and she drew a blank. No one, it seemed, remembered seeing the woman anywhere during the morning. The nurses couldn't recall when they saw her last, and Kay imagined that she had been the last person to see Mrs. Grover. But she went out into the grounds and made a thorough search, not ceasing until she was really certain the woman was not somewhere around. Then she went back to her office and telephoned the information to Miss Stokes.

"All I can do," Matron said when she had heard Kay's report, "is call the police in Cragton and give her description to them. If she is in town then they'll find her. Of course she is at liberty to go out, now she's so very much better, but she ought to have told us where she was going."

Kay agreed, and hung up. She went back to her duties, but there were nagging thoughts in the back of her mind.

During the afternoon Robin Kent approached her, and there was a grim expression on his face. Kay felt her heart miss a beat when she saw him, and she felt sure he was about to tell her that something dreadful had happened. But he was obviously suffering from his conscience, and Kay had no time for him when she learned that he was sorry for himself.

"She must have overheard me talking," he said in answer to her anxious question. "I'll never be able to live this down, if anything happens to her."

Kay said nothing, but as the afternoon wore on and there was no word of Mrs. Grover she became even more agitated. She blamed herself for not going along to Mrs. Grover's room immediatley she suspected that the woman had overheard Robin Kent. A few soothing words at the right moment might have settled the matter. She recalled that she had prevented Robin from going to talk to Mrs. Grover. She knew the woman was capable of anything in her present mental frame, and the worst possible fears were beginning to form in her mind.

Tea came and went, and Mrs. Grover did not reappear. When it was time for Kay to go off duty she handed over to her relief, then went along to Matron's office, finding the woman there as she expected, and Miss Stokes was very worried as she bade Kay enter her office. Kay hardly needed to ask the question that was on her lips. It was obvious from the other's manner that no word of their missing patient had come through.

"The police reported some minutes ago that there is no sign of Mrs. Grover, or anyone resembling her description, in town," Miss Stokes said. "I just don't know what to do now, Sister. The police fear that she may have wandered on to the moors instead of making her way to town. If that is the case then she could be anywhere."

"Are the police going to mount a search?" Kay demanded.

"A limited one to start with. She may turn up at any time, and the police seem to favour this idea."

"I don't think she will," Kay retorted. "It's

234

fairly obvious now that she overheard Dr. Kent's remarks, and she's taken it to heart." She sighed heavily. "I'm off duty now. I think I'll go out and start my own search for her."

"But there's such a large area to search. You could walk around the moors for a week and not find her."

"I'll get someone to drive me," Kay said.

She left the office and went back to the Sister's office, calling Martin at Cameron Glen, and as soon as he heard what the situation was he agreed to come and pick her up. She went up to her room to change out of her uniform, and there was no time to have tea. By the time she was ready to go out, Martin was arriving. She saw his car coming along the drive, and hurried down to the terrace to be there when he reached the building.

Martin got out of his car when he stopped near the terrace steps, and he came hurrying to where Kay was standing, his action making her pause to stare at him.

"There's a woman on the roof," he said sharply.

"A woman on the roof!" Kay turned instinctively and looked up at the front of the building, and her heart seemed to freeze when she saw a figure sitting on a flat, oblong stone that jutted out above the gable. There was a bare flag pole standing starkly beside the stone, and Kay could see one of the figure's arms raised slightly, the hand grasping the pole.

"Is that the missing woman?" Martin demanded, and his voice forced away some of the paralysis that held Kay.

She looked keenly at the figure, and nodded slowly. "It's Mrs. Grover," she said.

"How do we get up to the roof?" Martin put a hand upon Kay's arm and shook her gently.

"Inside," she gasped. "Up in the attic there are steps leading out to a flat part of the roof."

Martin started forward, and Kay hurried to his side, leading the way, pushing open the front door and hurrying along the corridor towards the stairs. One of the nurses on duty came by, and Kay paused and took hold of the girl's arm.

"Get Dr. Kent and Miss Stokes," she said quickly. "Tell them to come up to the roof. Mrs. Grover is up there. Don't raise any alarm, but get them as quickly as you can."

The nurse paled as she took in what Kay said, then she nodded and hurried away. Kay started up the stairs, and she was soon breathless. Martin kept at her side, silent and apprehensive, and when they reached the attic he took hold of Kay's hand.

"We've got to be very careful," he said. "If she's up on that jutting stone with the intention of throwing herself off then the slightest distraction might send her down."

"I have her confidence, if anyone has," Kay said, steeling herself. "Let me talk to her, Martin."

He nodded and led the way up the stairs that led to the flat roof, opening the door at the top and ushering Kay through it. Kay took a deep breath as she went forward to where the edge of the roof had a rail. The gable protruded beyond the rail, and there was a narrow catwalk along the gable, which gave access to the flag pole. Mrs. Grover was still seated on the jutting stone, and she was as motionless as a statue. Kay reached the rail and clutched at it. She could see the ground far below on her left, and her senses reeled as she felt the space between begin to pull at her. Martin came quietly to her side.

"Call her gently," he suggested in a whisper.

Kay nodded, gulping at the lump which had suddenly come into her throat. Her hands were trembling and she gripped the rail until her knuckles showed white.

"Mrs. Grover," she called. "This is Sister Latimer. Don't turn around or move. Just tell me that you're feeling all right."

There was no reply, and a tense moment passed while they waited for the woman to acknowledge their presence. The gable protruded twenty feet out from the edge where Kay was standing. The narrow wooden catwalk along the point of the roof seemed old and flimsy, and Kay suddenly felt sick with stifling fear. But she set her teeth into her bottom lip as she waited.

"Call her again," Martin said, and Kay obeyed, with no more success than the first time. "How long do you think she's been up here?" he demanded.

"She's been missing since before lunch," Kay said.

"Good Lord! Surely she hasn't been here all the time."

"We couldn't find her anywhere in the Clinic." Kay took a deep breath. She could feel her senses whirling as she felt space drawing at her. She didn't have a particularly strong stomach for this sort of thing. Heights had always left her feeling shaky and cold. But Mrs. Grover was her patient, and that made it a different matter. "Mrs. Grover," she called again. "Are you all right?"

She knew her words were ridiculous. The woman wouldn't be in that terrifying spot if she were all right. But she had to say something, to try and reassure the woman and

238

prevent the ultimate tragedy.

There was movement at her side and she glanced round to see Robin Kent coming breathless to her side. He stared out at Mrs. Grover and his face went white. He looked at Kay with a glazed expression in his brown eyes.

"Good God!" he ejaculated. "How long has she been out there?"

"That doesn't matter now," Martin retorted from his position on the other side of Kay. "The thing is to get her in before anything happens."

"Is she threatening to jump?" Kent demanded.

"She hasn't acknowledged our presence yet," Kay told him.

"I'll go out to her." Kent started to duck under the rail and reach for the catwalk with a hesitant foot.

"I wouldn't do that if I were you," Kay said quickly, placing a hand upon his shoulder. "It's because of you that she's out there, I do believe."

"You're kidding!"

"I told you she might have overheard your remarks. Don't go out there. You can only aggravate the situation."

"Well something's got to be done to help her," Kent said angrily.

His loud voice must have got through Mrs. Grover's daze, for the woman turned her head to look at them. Kay was shocked by the haggard expression which she saw, and even at that distance she could see a blankness in the dark eyes. But animation came into the gaunt face by slow degrees, and they all remained silent and still as they awaited developments.

"Doctor Kent, I never want to set eyes on you again or hear your voice," Mrs. Grover said in strangely wooden tones.

"Get out of here," Martin said firmly to Kent. "Turn round and walk away."

Robin Kent looked as if he would disagree, but Martin reached out a strong hand, took hold of the doctor's shoulder, and pulled him back behind the rail and sent him hurrying towards the door that led off the roof. At that moment Miss Stokes arrived, breathless and white-faced.

"Mrs. Grover," Matron said hurriedly. "Please come in off that ledge."

Kay placed a restraining hand upon Matron's arm, and when Mrs. Grover looked at them again, Kay asked:

"How long have you been out there, Mrs. Grover?"

"I don't know. I came up to the roof to be alone, to think over Dr. Kent's words. I thought he was deceiving me."

"It may have sounded like that, but I'm sure he didn't mean it that way." Kay tried to keep her tones even and calm, but she was cold inside, and trembling violently. "He's a very good doctor and he would do his best to help make your venture a great success. He was just talking generally when he mentioned that other business. You don't have to take any account of it."

"I don't know how I got out here," Mrs. Grover said slowly. "I was on the roof, and the next thing I know I was sitting out here."

"Would you like me to come and help you back to the roof?" Martin asked casually.

"Who are you?" Mrs. Grover demanded.

"I'm Martin Searle, a very good friend of Sister Latimer. I live in that big house you can see right over there. Can you see it?"

"It's a nice house. I'd like to buy one like that in Wales," Mrs. Grover said in child-like tones.

"Shall I come and help you in?" Martin repeated.

"I didn't come out to this position to throw myself off, if that's what you're thinking," Mrs. Grover said.

"I know that," Kay said quickly. "You've got so much to look forward to, Mrs. Grover. It's just that you've had such a serious breakdown, and perhaps all the excitement of the past two days, the pressures of making plans, have been just a little too much for you."

"Shall I come and help you in, Mrs. Grover?" Martin repeated.

"Yes please," came the immediate reply, "and please hurry. I'm afraid that I may fall."

"Keep very still." Martin glanced at Kay as he ducked under the rail. "I'm coming. Don't move at all and I'll get hold of you. You won't fall when I've got you. I'm not afraid of heights."

He stepped forward on to the catwalk as he spoke, and his weight caused a piece of rotting wood to break away. He swayed and almost lost his balance, and Kay gasped and leaned forward to grasp at his shoulder as she thought he was going to pitch off the roof. But he glanced at her and shook his head. His face was rather white, but he seemed not afraid.

"It'll be all right," he said quickly. "Stay there, Kay."

She nodded, almost speechless in fright, and she watched him go forward again. He moved slowly, testing the woodwork with his feet as he progressed.

"I'm coming towards you, Mrs. Grover,"

he said cheerfully. "I shall be close to you in a moment. But don't turn round and don't look down."

Kay watched intently, fearful and apprehensive. This seemed like a nightmare come true, she thought remotely. She saw Martin reach Mrs. Grover, heard him talking cheerfully to her, and watched him bend and take hold of the woman under the arms. He lifted her slowly and put an arm around her waist, holding her feet above the catwalk, and then he turned and came steadily back to where Kay was standing.

The next few moments would stay imprinted on Kay's mind for the rest of her life. But Martin made no mistakes with his feet and soon Kay was able to reach out and grasp Mrs. Grover's outstretched hand. The next instant they were both safely under the rail and standing on the flat roof. Mrs. Grover immediately burst into tears and subsided into Kay's arms, sobbing helplessly. Robin Kent appeared and took charge.

Mrs. Grover went down with Kent and Matron holding her, and Kay looked into Martin's face when they were alone on the roof.

"That was a very brave thing you did, Martin," she said shakily, and he laughed and took her into his arms. "But it was a good

243

job you're not afraid of heights! I'm petrified of them."

"I could tell that as soon as I looked into your face," he retorted, grinning faintly. "And so am I, Kay." He held up a hand for them both to see, and it was trembling violently. "I daren't even climb a short ladder."

"But you said –!" She broke off and stared into his face with growing concern. But admiration was beginning to break through in her eyes.

"She was your patient," he said softly. "I knew when Kent couldn't get near her that you would have to go, and I wasn't prepared to stand by and watch that, so I made myself do it."

"You're a hero, Martin," she whispered, her eyes shining. "To go out there knowing you were afraid of heights."

"A hero?" He chuckled. "Nothing so gallant, I'm afraid. I just happen to be in love with you. I would rather risk my neck than yours. That's all there was to it."

"That's more than sufficient," she said. "If you love me enough to risk your life to save mine then I'm going to be very humble for the rest of my life."

"Don't be humble." He took her into his arms and kissed her gently. "Just love me,

Kay. That's all I ask."

"I couldn't love you any more than I do already." She pressed her face against his shoulder and closed her eyes, feeling quite weak as reaction set in. But she knew all was well, and would continue in that direction.

"Come on," he said. "Don't let's stand here. We've got some celebrating to do. It's our anniversary, remember?"

"I had forgotten, as it happened," she said with a little sigh. "But I have a feeling that the rest of our lives will be one long celebration."

"And so it will," he told her. Then he kissed her and there was no need for words.

The evening sun shone palely upon them, and there was a lilt in the air. Spring was still very young, but growing stronger all the time, and so was their love . . .